Praise for *Dece*

In the slow, skillful development of the relationship between these two men, Strassberg plays on the initial gimmick of having Jesus and Santa analogues meet, and steadily broadens the story into a more ambitious meeting of the minds, drawing on elements of philosophy... An intense novella of ideas that looks into the heart of faith and generosity."

— Kirkus Reviews

•••

Adam Strassberg dives into the deep end of human experience. He is unafraid of any subject, especially the ones most of us avoid: religion, sex, politics, money, mental health, and our deepest fears about who we are. In *December on 5C4*, Adam reinterprets common mythology with humor and depth, inviting us to understand mental illness and our shared stories in a new way. You might experience him as either a dangerous heretic or an insightful oracle. I think he may be both.

— Rev. David Howell, Senior Minister, First Congregational Church of Palo Alto, UCC

•••

A unique tale for these times, where someone who might be Jesus meets someone who might be Santa on a psych ward at Christmas. Drawing from myth, religion, experience, and imagination, Adam Strassberg takes us on a tale that is both familiar and not, until we reach an end of hope and love. It is a Christmas story worth reading again and again.

— The Reverend Beth Neel, Presbytery of the Cascades

•••

Adam Strassberg's novella, *December on 5C4*, is infused with deep religious knowledge, expert understanding of the experience of delusions and voices in one's head, and humor, which together entice the reader to keep turning the pages. The story weaves together Jewish and Catholic teachings, elements of the Christmas holiday, and the pain of mental illness, poverty, and homelessness. The richly detailed narrative presents engaging discussions of the nature of God and life-guiding ethics while bringing to life its characters, settings, events, the spiritual world, and the Christmas fable. A most enjoyable read for the Holidays or anytime.

— Lorrin Koran, M.D., Professor of Psychiatry and Behavioral Sciences, Stanford Medical Center

Josh, a homeless Jewish apostate who hears the voice of God, spends Christmas in a psychiatric hospital after a spat with his boyfriend. There he meets Nick, a cocaine-addicted capitalist Santa-analogue whose belligerent jollity proves the biggest challenge yet to Josh's faith. Together, they hatch a plot to escape from the ward and get each other back on the right track.

With this culture clash of a story, Adam Strassberg has achieved a Christmas miracle. It's about mental illness and religion and addiction and love and loneliness - but the real miracle is that it never feels heavy; it never feels disrespectful. Quite the opposite: it's funny, sensitive, thought-provoking. The misfit characters are full of delightful contradictions. The prose is well researched; quotable; fizzing with vitality. It builds to a tense climax, and kept me guessing right to the end. One of the most refreshingly original things I've read in a long time."

— Charlie Fish, Editor-in-Chief of *Fiction on the Web*

• • •

Adam Strassberg's novella, *December on 5C4*, is infused with deep religious knowledge, expert understanding of the experience of delusions and voices in one's head, and humor, which together entice the reader to keep turning the pages. The story weaves together Jewish and Catholic teachings, elements of the Christmas holiday, and the pain of mental illness, poverty, and homelessness. The richly detailed narrative presents engaging discussions of the nature of God and life-guiding ethics while bringing to life its characters, settings, events, the spiritual world, and the Christmas fable. A most enjoyable read for the Holidays or anytime.

— Lorrin Koran, M.D., Professor of Psychiatry and Behavioral Sciences, Stanford Medical Center

• • •

Adam Strassberg is subtle and perceptive in immersing us into the experiences of two men, each bound on doing good, admitted to the psychiatric ward 5C4. In the guise of a Chanukkah/Christmas story, we are given insights into the predicaments, the spiritual joy, the inner peace, the doubting torments and the attraction of a God-inspired mind discovering the realities of the secular world. Written from knowledge of ritual, liturgy and professional experience, with distinctive humor, Strassberg succeeds in imparting meaning to awkward and absurd situations, leaving us thoughtful and inspired.

— Regina Casper, Professor of Psychiatry, Stanford University School of Medicine

December on 5C4

December on 5C4

Adam Strassberg

NAT 1 PUBLISHING
a literary nonprofit corporation
Books that make you question your choices.

This is a work of fiction. Names, characters, places, and incidents are products of the author's imagination or are used fictitiously and are not to be construed as real. Any resemblance to actual events, locales, organizations, or persons—living, dead, or immortal—is entirely coincidental.

DECEMBER ON 5C4
Copyright © 2024 by Adam Strassberg
Produced by Nat 1 Publishing, a literary nonprofit
www.nat1publishing.com
All rights reserved
v.1: 12.01.2024

ISBN: 9798337610870

Cover Art, Edits, and Design by B.S.Roberts
Title/Heading Font: "Beyond Wonderland" by Chris Hansen
Interior Font: "EB Garamond 12" by Georg Duffner

No part of this book may be reproduced or used in any manner without the written permission of the copyright holder or Nat 1 Publishing, except for the use of quotations in a book review. The scanning, uploading, and distribution of this book without permission from the publisher are illegal and punishable by law. Please purchase only authorized editions—your support of the author's rights is appreciated.

Opinions expressed in this publication are those of the author. They do not purport to reflect the opinions or views of the publishing house or its members. The publisher does not have any control over and does not assume any responsibility for author or third-party websites, social media, or their content.

*For gift givers,
everywhere and everywhen*

December on 5C4

JOSH FROWNED.

This time, he had really messed up. The only thing worse than spending the holiday locked on 5C4 is spending a birthday locked on 5C4. And Josh knew now he would have to endure both.

He was awake but not woken. His mind moved, but his body refused to budge. One vinyl pillow covered his eyes, and the other muffled his ears. His large nose periscoped upwards above the covers, and thick nostrils flared. He breathed. Slowly, just as Dr. Fischman had recommended during his last admission: Slow deep breath in—1, 2, 3—and hold—slow deep breath out. Repeat.

With each breath, there came odors. An alphabet of smells: alcohol, bleach, chlorine, feces, gel, iodine, lamisil, paint, smoke, talc, urine, vomit. This was the aroma of ward 5C4, all too familiar to Josh, and all too fetid. There was an earnest scent of disinfectant, but it was easily overcome by the smell of disease mixed with the stench of homelessness. He sniffed some less familiar tones, too. Burnt coffee, cold fryer oil, melting popsicles, stale popcorn, warm lemonade. At least this time his room was near the floor canteen.

Josh woke. Innocent yet familiar words of gratitude stirred from his consciousness. He whispered the traditional morning prayer: **Modeh anee lefanecha melech chai vekayam, she-he-chezarta bee nishmatee b'chemla, raba emunatecha.** *I offer thanks to You, living and eternal King, for You have mercifully restored my soul within me; Your faithfulness is great.* Since his departure from the community, it had been easy to shed the rules but much harder to shed these rituals.

Josh lay still, supine, upon his cot. The mattress had the familiar lumpiness of cheap foam beneath a zippered plastic cover. After a bit more, he rallied his strength and rolled to one side. Movement of any kind had become so hard over these last few weeks. He had become, again, just so slow and sluggish. As Josh rolled his body, the vinyl pillow fell from over his face, and he struggled to open his eyelids. He saw first the wood laminate of his bed frame, then further on the bricked walls of his room, coated with layers of fresh gray paint. He next looked down at the matching gray carpet, then up to the two small windows on the far wall just beneath the ceiling. Outside, beneath a distant opaque sky, snowflakes fell.

That was the last thing Josh remembered: snowflakes, and right before that, his big fight with Yehud. "You need to choose, Josh—you can be a self-hating Jew or a self-hating faggot - but you can't be both!" Yehud had yelled, but the God voice in Josh's head was louder. Too loud then, and too fast. It talked in circles, spirals, and endless contradictions. It proclaimed God's love but also warned of God's wrath. There were rewards in Heaven, but also punishments on Earth. The voice commanded him to love everyone equally, which was impossible to obey. He loved Yehud too much, and so he was being selfish. Josh's speech had slowed. He remembers feeling hungry, fasting, feeling frenetic, but sleeping. How had it become so easy to feel yet so hard to think? His mind was filled with questions that his heart could not understand. It all felt off now, somehow. Yet whenever he held Yehud, the feeling was always good, kind, and patient. The God voice did not care either way, it just boomed and bellowed, too fast and then too loud.

Yehud screamed at Josh, then slapped him. "It's been almost six weeks! I've had enough. Everyone has. Nothing you preach to us makes sense anymore!" Yehud threw a small red bag of coins down at Josh's feet. "I'll be camping over at Kever Garden. Meet me there outside by the big rock on your birthday." He lifted his full backpack and snapped the straps. "I'll have a cake for you with thirty-three candles; come to blow them out, or don't come at all." He gave Josh one last long open-mouthed kiss before turning away, riding off barefoot on his banana bike despite the flat tire.

Josh just stood there in the middle of the street. He felt a huge ache in his right side as he watched Yehud cycle away. *Father in Heaven, please end this suffering. I love you, but I love him. Choose another, any other would be more worthy. Please leave me. Please let me live an ordinary mortal life.* He stood frozen, staring at their few remaining tents in Godsmane Park. It was a small abandoned green space near the freeway overpass by the edge of the old Oil Press Neighborhood. In the center of their encampment, twelve broken chairs surrounded one large cardboard box, atop it were scattered fish bones, moldy bread pieces, cut flowers, and several empty wine bottles. Nobody was there. *Where is everyone? I am a **rebbe** with no **bochurim**. Have they all forsaken me?*

Josh walked up the freeway overpass and on into the traffic. He slowed down but his world had sped up. The God voice echoed in his head. His memory fogged. The cops must have come, they always did. He remembered his wrists tied again in plastic cables. Then there was his usual social worker, Ms. Longini,

December on 5C4

from the Mental Health Crisis team. A single short-acting involuntary injection, and he was on medications again. Her voice soothed him as he fell asleep. She reminded him that he would be safe in 5C4, safe for the winter holiday, and safe over his birthday.

And now he had awoken.

Good morning, 5C4, guten morgen.

At least it felt like morning. Josh closed his eyes, bit down slowly on his lip, then lurched his torso upward and his feet downward. He landed in a sitting position on his cot and now could see the rest of his room. He was in a double, but with no roommate yet, as the second bed was empty. A large round clock was cemented into the wall behind the two cots, above and between them. A small sink with a mirror was centered on the opposite wall. Josh rose stiffly and shuffled towards the mirror. A familiar blue paper was taped next to the mirror:

"*Involuntary Patient Advisement,* form DHCS 1802 ... You are being placed into this psychiatric facility because it is our professional opinion, that as a result of a mental health disorder, you are likely to: ✓ harm yourself, ☐ harm someone else, ☐ be unable to take care of your own food clothing or shelter ... We believe this is true because: "multiple witnesses reported you running onto a freeway, yelling, and hitting your head with your fists" ... You will be held for a period of up to 72 hours."

So much for the holiday, so much for my birthday, so much for freedom.

Josh placed both hands on the side of the sink basin and leaned toward the oval mirror. He stared into it, a young man stared out. *Or maybe not so young*, he considered. *Am I really turning thirty-three tomorrow?* He rotated his face and inspected it, still no wrinkles. He had a round Ashkenazi face, but his skin was a smooth olive-brown, betraying the Sephardic heritage on his mother's side. Oval brown eyes bordered each side of a very large aquiline nose framed by thick nostrils. Below this, his mouth was wide with thin lips. He opened his mouth and inspected the teeth with his tongue. Unlike most of his followers, his were all still there, and from the minty taste, someone must have recently brushed them.

That same someone, too, must have trimmed the scraggles from his long brown beard. And cleaned and cut his fingernails. And even his toenails? He looked down at his feet, now in sandals. His feet had been washed, his hair too; his whole body actually. He could feel the delousing powder beneath his white hospital pajamas. He remembered very little from between his fight with Yehud and his awakening just now. That nurse Magda must have been on shift during his intake.

He stood up on his toes, stretched, then placed his heels back down. He was average height, at least for a **haredim**—maybe five feet and five inches—but considered short now that he lived amongst the **goyim**. He took his hands and roped his long brown hair up and back into a layered top knot. After he wandered off the **derech**, off the path, he could never bring himself to cut his **payot**. He preferred to keep his sidelocks. He liked the cozy feel of them unwrapped and untucked, and so he grew all of his other hair much longer to match.

He took a step back and returned to staring into the mirror. *Who am I?* A man in white pajamas stared back, lovingly. It was an image at once both familiar and alien. *A son of Adam,* **ben adam,** *of course, beloved by God, but who isn't? A* **chasid** *once, one of the righteous, who was now most anything but. Meshuggener, faygelah, heymloz, shonda. Crazy, gay, homeless, disgraced.* His parents had long ago torn their shirts and sat **shiva**.

The buttons on his pajama top were misaligned. Josh flapped open the shirt to unbutton, then re-button, the column. He noticed the old scar on his right chest, but also now the curves of muscles. He had been so much fatter before his time on the streets. He tucked the white pajama shirt into the matching elastic pants, then flattened out the outfit. He felt a sticker over the chest pocket on his shirt. This name tag had his first name with the initial of his last written with black marker. He was mostly "Josh" on the streets but remained "Yeshua N." in the hospital records.

Josh plugged the drain, then ran the faucet and filled half the sink with water. This would be his morning purification. He placed his right hand beneath the water up to the wrist, then removed it and dunked his left hand similarly. He repeated one more time, right, then left. He recited the ancient chant softly, "Blessed are you, O Lord, our God, King of the Universe, who has sanctified us through your commandments and has commanded us concerning the washing of hands." In Hebrew, this was the **Netilat Yadayim,** in Yiddish, the *Negel Vasser*, in English, the Hand Uplifting. Josh spoke all three languages fluently, though his favorite language was the unspoken one—love. It was at once universal and useful, primal and inchoate, yet also the apex of all human needs and desires.

Josh dried his hands as the water circled down the sink drain. He felt an unfamiliar dull pain in his belly. Was he hungry? He could not remember his last meal. He must be hungry. He *loved* that he was hungry. He needed food, and he desired to get it. He would break his fast. Then, as if on cue, a two-tone preamble trumpeted through the ward PA system, followed by a young woman's voice: "Rise and shine, everyone. Today is going to be a great day. Breakfast is served now in the canteen."

December on 5C4

HE HEARD THE FAT MAN long before he saw him. Josh left his room and shuffled down the hallway towards the canteen. After so many hospitalizations on 5C4, he was familiar with both the floor plan and the meal plan.

"Ho, ho, ho!" The deep laughter clearly arose from the depths of a large man's belly, surfacing in long well-spaced sputters. "Ha, ha, ha!"

Josh continued toward the canteen. The main hallway had twelve dorm rooms, mostly doubles with two singles, and ended in a large common room where six round tables were placed during meals. The canteen itself was not a separate space, but rather just a converted wall to one side of the common room—a long bar crossed the middle of that wall, with a food service window above. It was opened during mealtimes but otherwise kept closed by a metal security shutter that rolled down and locked. A bench nearby held coffee, tea, hot chocolate, lemonade, and packaged snacks.

Josh heard a deep voice, one which matched that deep laugh. "What do you call a selfish elf?" No one offered a guess. "Nobody. Really. *Myyss-elf!*" Then, another round of deep laughter. "Ho, ho, ho! Ha, ha, ha!"

Josh surprised himself with a small smile. He had not smiled in weeks. *That was pretty silly… and that laugh… how could anyone have so much energy this early in the morning? And how could anyone be so jolly here on 5C4?*

There was no line for breakfast as Josh was last to arrive. He walked toward the canteen and took his meal tray from the orderly. He turned to the tables; only one open chair remained at the far table next to the tall, fat man who was sitting with no meal tray. Josh shuffled over and sat down across from him.

"It's okay little buddy, you go ahead and eat. My breakfast is comin'." The man shifted his torso side to side, lifted his knees up and down, and tapped his feet and fingers, all to a beat only he seemed to feel.

Josh's plate held a mix of toasted bread, blueberry muffins, powdered eggs, fried tomatoes, canned fruit, and an orange drink. It would be the first real meal he had eaten in weeks. Also, the most varied, as what he found on the streets somehow was always just leftover bread, fish, or wine. Josh lowered his head and folded his hands, then mumbled several **brachot rishonot**—blessings before eating—for the various foods on his tray. He grabbed his fork and prepared to eat his meal.

"You mumble a lot, huh. You're one of the quiet ones. I'm one of the loud ones." The man cupped his hands over his ears and exaggerated a silly squint. "Hey, do you know where they put the loudest elf?"

Josh shrugged his shoulders.

"On the *shhhh-elf!*" The fat man slapped his hands onto the table, rattling Josh's meal tray. "Ho, ho, ho! Ha, ha, ha!"

The man spoke with an accent. It was slight, hard to place, a bit Eastern European, perhaps Slavic, somewhat akin to Josh's father's lilt. The man also resembled his father physically. Except for the height, at six feet or more, this man was much taller, but he was equally as fat, with a large belly and a pear-shaped midriff. Somehow, he wore deep red pajamas, though the standard issue for 5C4 was white. He was fair skinned with a broad face. He seemed late middle-aged from the crow's feet wrinkles to the sides of his twinkling eyes. A pair of round spectacles balanced atop his button cherry-like nose. He had dimples, a small mouth, and rosy cheeks, with a long, well-groomed white beard. His head was otherwise bald, again like Josh's father, however, with no **kippah** atop and no **payot** wrapped around his ears. There were also no thin **talit katan** tassels dangling beneath this man's pajama shirt.

The man pointed to the name tag on his shirt. "My name tag says Topher K., but everyone calls me Nick. It's my nickname. Get it? Nick-name!" He slapped the table again. His heavy silver wedding ring rang the tabletop like a bell.

Josh's drink nearly spilled. "Sir, could you please—" He began but was interrupted by that enormous laugh.

"Ho, ho, ho! Ha, ha, ha!" The fat man's belly shook whenever he laughed, like a bowl full of jelly.

An orderly entered the room with a large white bag from McDonald's. He gave Nick the bag, then walked behind the food service window and returned with a bottle of Coca-Cola, two small boxes of milk, and a large ceramic mug of hot chocolate. Nick slipped his hand into the breast pocket of his red pajama shirt, then slid out a rubber-banded roll of green bills. He unstrapped the roll, peeled off a C-note, gave it to the orderly, then rewrapped the roll and returned it to the bottom of his shirt pocket.

"I can't help it. I *Mclove it*, my *Mickie D's.*" He removed four Egg McMuffin sandwiches, four hash browns, and two large chocolate chip cookies from the bag. "Mostly though, I just love coke." He bit into his first sandwich and then popped the top off his tall bottle of Coca-Cola. "I am addicted to coke—to the great trinity of cokes: Coca-Cola, hot cocoa, and, of course, Mr. C. himself, the original, cocaine." He alternatively gulped his cola and chomped on his sandwiches. He spoke rapidly but loudly and clearly. "I adore snow! They say I was doing blow last night when it happened, but dust doesn't ramp me up at this point, anyway. I always have this much energy. I talk fast. I think fast. I live fast. Who needs sleep?"

Josh slowly scooped a small spoonful of his powdered eggs, swallowed, and then even more slowly scooped again. In the same span of time, the man ate all four sandwiches and hash browns and imbibed his soda. Nick then placed a straw into one milk box, unfolding open the other, into which he dunked one of the cookies. He took the second cookie and pushed it across the table toward Josh.

"Hey, little fella, would you like a gift? Here's a cookie." Nick offered this with a rapid but much softer and quieter voice.

"No, thank you."

"Oh, come on, take it, it's my gift to you. I love giving gifts," he insisted, his speech becoming louder and firmer.

Josh lifted his head from his tray and breathed in the fragrance of the freshly baked cookie. He thought of the dough, sugar, and chocolate all melting in his mouth. It had been so long since he had indulged in such an extravagance. But he remembered his vows, what he had learned from the God voice and his own teachings. "No, thank you." He lifted the palm of his right hand, then motioned toward the cookie. "Man does not live by bread alone, or in this case by cookie, but we live by every word that proceeds from the mouth of God."

"I knew it. You're one of those homeless hippies from over near the freeway." Nick grumbled, then took a long sip from his milk straw as his complexion turned redder and redder. His eyes narrowed, but then he laughed. "Ha, ha, ha! The joke's on me. I pay for private insurance through my company, and the first time I really need it, every real looney bin is full, and I get stuck in this county facility with all you zealots."

Josh's mind was still jumbled, his thoughts slow, his concentration dull. It would be hard to match the fat man's speed and alacrity, but Josh knew he had God. He closed his eyes and listened inside for that still, small voice, then he exhorted himself to speak whatever truths he could summon. "My group, my followers, we are not zealots though we do have zeal. It can be hard to understand—I have trouble with it myself." Josh forced a smile, then slowly lifted his eyes to meet Nick's gaze. "Our group, our path—it's a lifestyle, a way of being in the world. Our community is devoted to simplicity, peace, cooperation, and love. We share everything, our love, our labors, all with each other equally." Josh took a small sip of his orange drink and swallowed. "We are a community—we commune not just with God but with each other. For us, there is no ownership, no private or personal property." Josh pointed to the second cookie sitting on the table between them. "So, you see, I can't enjoy a cookie for myself when everyone else around me can't have one, too." The cookie appeared twice as large as before but not enough for everyone to share. "Our group—we take from this world only what little we need to survive, then give everything else to the poor. We are rich beyond measure, but our treasure lies in Heaven. We are never poor, but we do choose poverty."

"You mean you choose stupidity," the fat man snickered his response. "That's just childish. It's irresponsible! There's no virtue in choosing poverty; you're just choosing to suffer together pointlessly." Nick shook his head. "We all have an obligation to avoid our own poverty. We have a duty to one another, to each earn our own living through gainful employment." Nick lifted his index finger and pointed upward. "I assure you that's what your so-called God wants each of you to do. It's your responsibility to do everything in your power to avoid being a burden on others."

The other more meager conversations in the common room now ceased. A quiet rolled over any other voices as heads at other tables turned toward Nick, then Josh. "With respect, Nick, you are missing the point. God doesn't want our independence; he wants our interdependence."

"But your ideas just lead to dependence." Nick lifted the enlarged second cookie, then took a large bite and swallowed. "You say that man cannot live by bread alone, but man still has to have bread to live, so we need men to bake it. If everyone is a beggar, then who will bake the bread?" Nick stood up at the table and banged his fist.

Josh remained seated. He folded the fingers of his hands together and continued his smiling gaze toward Nick. "In the kingdom of Heaven, there will be neither rich nor poor, neither givers nor takers, donors nor beggars, for we are all one. It will be a world in which we labor together equally and then share equally in the results of our labors." As Josh talked, gray clouds in the sky outside the windows suddenly parted to reveal a blue sky behind them. A single ray of sunshine then beamed into the common room, touching Josh with a glow upon his shoulders and scalp.

An orderly pushed a small cart and began collecting meal trays. Nick remained standing and pointed toward the young man. "But then why labor at all? People are selfish. Workers are lazy—I know mine are. Where's the motivation?

In this heaven of yours, you might as well work as little as possible since you get the same share no matter what. So then nothing ever gets done, and we are all the poorer for it. Suddenly nobody has enough bread to eat because nobody is baking bread, because *why bother?*"

"Why not bother? Capitalism has failed us. It has enslaved us with chains none can see, but all can feel. Our patriarch Moshe told the enslaved they were free. I can only imagine how difficult that was. But I have been commanded to tell people who think they are free that they are enslaved. God demands it. This has been my path, and it is much more difficult. I think it might be impossible." Josh sighed. "I don't claim to understand it or that any of it makes sense. My followers believe I hear God, or at least that what I teach is God's word. It's not logical. I don't know if any of it is true, but it feels true."

Four patients stood behind Josh, another four behind Nick. The crowd was split.

Nick continued: "Should I be locked up right now? Should you? Should any of us? Is that logical? Does it *feel* true? But here we are locked up, all of us, and that is the truth." He finished the second cookie, then smacked and slapped his hands together as if shaking off dirt. "Something *feeling true* doesn't *make it true*. It may *feel* true that people are equal, but people are *not* equal. We have different abilities. Some of us are just better than others. And some of us make out better than others. I worked hard to earn my money. I took risks. I used my talents." Nick turned from Josh's gaze and looked toward the wall, yelling at no one in particular, "Why should I be forced to give away what I earned to other people?"

"Nick, we each give to the government what is the government's, and to God what is God's."

"That's easy to say when you have nothing to give. You're homeless—" the fat man took his fingers and made air quotes. "Sorry, *houseless*, or whatever you all want to call yourselves. I know if you've been bad or good, and you've all been bad. My tax dollars go to pay for the land where you illegally squat in your tents. You take a shared community space and selfishly hog it all for yourselves, all the while pretending to be selfless. The streets fill up with your noise, graffiti, and garbage. It's dirty, disgusting, and threatening out there. You can't walk a city block without being assaulted by a randomly screaming drug addict or a jabbering unmedicated psycho." Nick kept speaking louder and faster. He stood across from Josh at the table and began pounding his fists together. "You people claim to choose poverty, but what you really choose is to impoverish the rest of us. You choose not to take medications that you should, and you choose to use street drugs that you shouldn't. You choose homelessness—or 'houselessness' or whatever— but it's really just all about being lawless."

Josh's speech remained soft and slow. He was either unaffected or unaware of Nick's agitation. Perhaps both. "We are not lawless; we just don't follow Man's laws, only God's laws." His words echoed against the walls of the room. A faint sound of bells—or perhaps it was the walls themselves—could be heard chiming. The melody was eerie and ephemeral, somehow both unrecognizable yet familiar. "It's impossible for a wealthy man to enter the Kingdom of Heaven. It'd be easier to drive a car through a keyhole than for someone rich to enter God's kingdom. The rich must surrender their wealth to the poor; only then can they have treasure in Heaven. Because money makes it hard to be a good person, to be closer to God. You can't serve two masters. Either you will hate one and love the other, or you will be devoted to the one and despise the other. You cannot serve both God and money."

"Ho, ho, ho! Ha, ha, ha!" Nick placed both hands on the sides of his belly and shook himself forward and back in a sudden fit of laughing. "That's just dumb." He was laughing but also crying. *Of course you can serve both*. I do. I love giving gifts to people. But it's impossible to give to charity if one *is* a charity." He grabbed a napkin from the table, wiped his tears, then blew his nose. He continued loudly, "And by far, my most charitable gift is what I offer to my workers—well-paid jobs with benefits. This is the highest form of charity, *a partnership*. We partner with them so they can support themselves, they learn autonomy."

"Or just to be automatons," Josh rebuked, sitting calmly, then allowed himself to reconsider. "I'm sorry." He had lost himself in argument, by arguing. "I'm sorry that we disagree."

Nick was trembling. His hands were clenched into fists, and his skin had turned a dark red. A nurse entered the room with two large orderlies at her sides. All three slowly approached Nick from behind, then paused as Josh finished his apology.

"Maybe we can agree on other things?" Josh closed his eyes and searched within, reminding himself how God blesses the peacemaker. "You love giving gifts. Well, I love giving gifts too. Gifts spread joy."

More clouds outside in the sky parted, and the sunbeam shining down on Josh's shoulders and scalp quickly expanded and brightened. Josh, Nick, their table, the patients surrounding them, the nurse, and the orderlies all shimmered beneath this sudden burst of sunlight.

Nick stepped back from the table as each orderly approached him from the sides. He nodded a silent agreement to walk out behind the nurse.

The God voice had always commanded Josh to love everyone, but it never insisted that he like everyone. Not everyone was likable, especially this fat man, and not everyone liked Josh, particularly this fat man. At such times, Josh found comfort in prayer. He prayed for anyone who disliked him or whom he disliked— or both.

"Nick, may I pray for you?" Josh asked.

Nick turned his head, giggled, then scratched the tip of his nose with his middle finger. "Sure, whatever. But answer this riddle first— what's the rudest type of elf?"

Josh shrugged his shoulders.

Nick was escorted back to his room for some brief *isolation* and *de-escalation*, but managed one last yell from the hallway: "The *Gofuckyours-elf!*"

WARD POLICY was that both patients involved in any heated argument or altercation must complete *isolation* and *de-escalation* protocols. And so, after Nick was escorted to his "time out," the staff asked Josh—albeit more politely and with an odd deference—if he would please return to his room as well.

Josh was still hungry but complied. He left his breakfast nearly uneaten. He had not taken in more than a **kezayit** of his meal, so he had no need to recite any **brachot acharonot**, the blessings after eating. He did, however, pause to offer a *mi shebeirach* for Nick.

He lowered his eyes and mumbled this traditional Jewish prayer for healing as he returned to his room. He concentrated on Nick and focused on his soul as he quickly spoke the holy words.

Mi Sheberach Avoteinu: Avraham, Yitzhak, v'Yaakov, v'Imoteinu: Sarah, Rivka, Rachel v'Leah, Hu yivarech virapei et hacholeh, Nick o Topher K. HaKadosh Baruch Hu yimalei rachamim alav, l'hachalimo, u-l'rap'oto, l'hachaziko, u-l'chay-oto/u-l'chay-otah. V'yishlach lo/lah bimhera r'fuah shlemah, r'fu-at hanefesh u-r'fu-at hagoof, b'toch sh'ar cholei Yisrael v'cholei yoshvei tevel, hashta ba'agalah u-vizman kariv, v'no-mar, Amen!

May the One who blessed our ancestors—Abraham, Isaac, and Jacob, Sarah, Rebecca, Rachel, and Leah—bless and heal the one who is ill, Nick or Topher K. May the Holy Blessed One overflow with compassion upon him, to restore him, to heal him, to strengthen him, to enliven him. The One will send him, speedily, a complete healing—healing of the soul and healing of the body—along with all the ill, among the people of Israel and all humankind, soon, speedily, without delay, and let us all say: Amen!

When we pray for other people, those are the prayers that God loves best. So though his room remained mostly quiet, as his prayer ended, Josh heard the blaring of trumpets and a brief loud chorus of angelic voices. He looked through the two windows atop his wall and saw the sky fill again with dark clouds. The wind blew and whistled against the glass. Snowflakes began to fall.

December on 5C4

He shuffled toward his bed. Before he could lie down, he was intercepted by a young nursing assistant. "Mr. N.? You forgot to get your medication." She held his hand and led him out of his room and down the hallway. Other patients were now strolling the hallway toward their dorm rooms, leaving the common room as staff transformed it from mealtime to break time, then to group time set-ups. Josh and the aide walked together down the hallway and past several of these rooms; some had doors open, others closed, and many now held men and women in various states of distress or de-stress, all wearing white pajamas except, apparently, for Nick.

The door to Nick's room was closed, but Josh could tell it was his from the loud argument within as they passed. His voice was so deep and distinctive, "So if I agree to take your stupid pill, then I can get out of here? Cause I got places to be!" But there were other voices behind other doors and inside other doorways as well. A cacophony of punctuated yelps, screams, sobs, and cries played as Josh and the nursing assistant traipsed down the long hallway. It ended in a dark wooden chair with tan cushions to the side of a large black door. The aide beckoned Josh to sit, then knocked three times on the door, turned, and left.

The large black door was, in fact, two smaller black half-doors, hung one atop the other. The top door swung inward to reveal a large closet with shelf upon shelf of medication jars. An attendant within reached outward to give Josh a small white paper cup. She then filled a somewhat larger paper cup with water from a cooler and handed this one to Josh as well.

Josh lifted the smaller paper cup to his mouth, then stopped himself. "My pill is usually a blue capsule, but this one is red. Are you sure this is right?"

"They say you need to relax from this morning, so this is what Dr. Fischman ordered."

Josh sat on the chair. He lifted the small paper cup with the red pill in one hand, he lifted the cup of water in his other hand. *We each give to God what is God's*, Josh mused. He quickly recited the prayer before taking medicine: **Yehi ratzon milfanecha, Ado-nai Elo-hai, she'yehai eisek zeh li li'refuah ki rofai chinam atta.** *May it be Your will, Lord my God, that this activity will bring healing to me, for You are the free Healer*— then swallowed his pill and drank the water.

The aide returned and led Josh back down the hallway to his dorm room. Her hand was delicate, her fingers soft against his own rough, calloused palm. She was his shepherd, and he was her sheep. His mind was fogging, and everything around him was becoming fuzzier and fluffier, more pastoral and pleasant. She unfurled a woolen blanket and placed it over Josh as he lay down, then tucked him in beneath it. He suddenly felt very sleepy. But still sad, ever so sad. He missed Yehud, and now he would never get a chance to see him again. He gazed up from his bed and out the two windows atop his bedroom wall. The sky outside unfurled a blanket as well. It was snowing heavily.

Josh wept.

He closed his eyes. He did not want to be here, locked on 5C4. Sometimes, he did not want to be anywhere. Perhaps he did not want to be at all? Then he remembered back to the last time he did. It had been snowing heavily that day, too.

It was sixteen years ago, perhaps to the day, when he and cousin Yochanan shared that moment at the *mikvah*. Their town was so proud of their *mikvah*. Most are fed by rainwater, some by natural springs, but they lived near enough to the riverside that their *mikvah* was fed by the living waters of the nearby river Yarden itself. The outside remained an unassuming city row house covered with dark vines and modest aging red brick. But the inside had been renovated and re-renovated over the years, built anew with each generation. The building was divided upon entry, with the men's facilities to the left, and the women's to the right. Each had first a large changing room, with lockers, seats, sinks, toilets, and an open shower. Both changing rooms led to the same single *mikvah* bath, which was open for women in the evenings and men in the afternoons and mornings.

Since his bar mitzvah, Josh had plunged into the *mikvah* before every *shabbos*. It was customary for men to purify themselves in this way in preparation for the sabbath. Whenever Josh stepped down into the *mikvah* waters, he was overcome by a sense of spiritual renewal and peacefulness. He immersed himself, then was cleansed of all sin and reborn. He would come to the bath to satisfy this deep quest for spiritual purity; he would linger, however, very much unsatisfied due to a deeper quest for something else. Something unnamable. This younger Josh would loiter in the locker room, both before and after his *tevilah*, glancing at the bodies of other teenage boys but never staring. He had no words for it, this yearning, though he needed no words to know it was a sin.

That Friday morning, Josh had arrived unusually early and there was also an unusual snowstorm, so both the locker room and *mikvah* were still empty. After cleaning and combing, Josh approached the door to the *mikvah* chamber when his cousin Yochanan appeared and opened it for him. He was Josh's second cousin, six months older than he, their mothers were first cousins and had grown up next door to one another. Everyone in the community was mostly related to everyone else, though the two mostly knew each other as classmates at *yeshiva*.

Josh held the silver railing and stepped down the stairs into the empty *mikvah* bath. It was a five-foot cubic inset in the center of the room. The larger chamber itself was circular, about twenty feet in diameter, windowless, but with a

December on 5C4

domed roof and a large skylight at its apex. The walls were molded into a smooth cobalt sandstone that melded into the floor, whose perimeter was lined by planter boxes filled with flowers and small bushes. Everything around the bath was warm and smelled of pine.

Josh stood in the center of the pool and submerged himself. The waters were cool without being cold. Josh emerged and recited the blessing: **"Barukh ata Adonai Elohenu melekh ha'olam asher kideshanu b'mitzvotav v'tzivanu al ha'tevillah."** *Blessed are You, O Lord, our God, King of the universe, who has sanctified us with Your commandments and commanded us concerning the immersion.*

"Amen," Yochanon startled Josh from behind. He was standing right there, his long camel hair coat, clothing, and shoes all bundled in a ball by the entrance. "I locked the doors so we could be alone," he turned to face Josh. "And safe."

Over the last few years, Josh and Yochanon had been holding glances far too often and far too long. They favored each other at the dances, grasping hands in the circles and clasping hands to shoulders in the lines. Naked in the bath together, their bodies told a truth to one another, which their mouths could never speak.

"The waters here will forgive us our **keri**." Yochanon beckoned, "The **mikvah** cannot be made **pasul**."

"We are immersed here in God's love," Josh agreed.

They were immersed, too, in their love for one another, as they explored, intertwined and pleasured each other. How could sin be so sweet? The forbidden, so unforgettable?

When it was over, they held one another, spooning in the shallow waters beneath the skylight. You can lie to yourself, but you cannot lie to the desires of your flesh. A sin requires choice, and there was none. For Josh, there was no state of **tumah**, spiritual impurity, and so he felt no **teshuva**, desire for repentance.

But Leviticus was clear: *"Thou shalt not lie with mankind, as with womankind; it is detestable." "And if a man lie with mankind, as with womankind, both of them have committed a detestable act: They shall surely be put to death; their blood shall be upon them."*

Josh wept.

Yochanon whispered, "Maybe I can prepare the way of the Lord for you, somehow purify you, so you can be right with God." He splashed water over his face. "I may be just a voice crying out in the wilderness, but please let me bless you." Yochanon placed both hands above Josh's head as Josh let himself be submerged again in the pool. His cousin then spoke an invocation: "I immerse you now, Yeshua, in the name of God; may He bless your body, heart, and spirit."

When Josh arose from the waters, both he and Yochanon were startled by a flock of pigeons squawking outside atop the skylight above them, somehow despite the snowstorm.

This was when Josh first heard the voice in his head. Was it the actual voice of God? It was still. It was small. But it was powerful. "You are my beloved son, in whom I am well pleased." Josh did not understand those words then, but he had unraveled them since, like a divine riddle. We are all God's perfect children, and he loves us all just as we are. When we love one another, however we love one another, God feels our love and smiles with us.

Josh understood then that he could never return home. He kissed Yochanon. It was a long and loving kiss followed by a longer, loving embrace.

They quickly unlocked the door and others soon arrived. Yochanon dressed and left first. Then Josh followed. He dressed, left the **mikvah**, then the community entirely. Josh walked straight south from their small town into the city center. He wandered off the **derech**, off the path, never looking back.

Josh smiled now, years later, in his bed on 5C4, as he relived again and again this sublime memory with Yochanon from so long ago. He comforted himself with familiar bible verses: *"I grieve for you, Yochanon my brother; you were very dear to me. Your love for me was wonderful, so very wonderful…"* Ruminations of long ago soon relaxed into just recollections, then these memories melted away into mindlessness as the morning medication pushed Josh into a very deep sleep.

December on 5C4

IV

MEN DREAM OF GOD, God dreams of men. Josh mostly just dreamt about himself. Though these dreams were never remembered, at least not over these last many years.

He did well at first. A cop found him asleep in the park that same snowy night long ago when he first left his community. The man was kind enough to bring him to a nearby shelter for teenage boys. Josh was legally still a "runaway minor," but that same officer also connected him with an organization called Footsteps, and they helped him petition for status as an "emancipated minor." His counselor there helped him transition with Section 8 assistance to more secure group housing and even start a job as a day laborer. He would come to the parking lot at 5AM, then the truck would drive them all to the construction site where Josh mostly worked assisting the framers. He and his father had enjoyed woodworking together in their scant free time outside of **Torah** studies and so Josh found that he loved helping the framers with their much larger wooden constructions. They erected walls out of studs and headers, laid floors from joists and beams, and framed roofs with poles and rafters. They paid minimum wage, but in cash, at 5PM each night before driving everyone back to a parking lot in the city. With enough hours, Josh hoped to start under the framers as an apprentice, perhaps someday even working his way up to the carpenters' union. The job site was also where he first met his new friend Yehud, another runaway, also off the **derech**. They began rooming together in the group house, at first sharing the same bed literally, out of common necessity to save rent money, then liberally, out of shared desires far beyond those of just friendship.

For those first six months, he had friends, unlike now, real actual friends, not just followers. At that point, he had only heard God's voice one time—that day in the **mikvah** with Yochanon.

But then, six months later, when he turned eighteen, something happened.

It started as a low intermittent whistle, then a mumble, a grumble, a murmur of unintelligible speech, until finally, he heard it again—God's voice.

Now, however, it commented continually and insufferably on all aspects of Josh's daily life. It had started as a warm and loving male voice but became colder and often grumpy. What's more, God *simply would not shut up*. He could not get God's voice—an actual, literal voice inside his head—to stop speaking.

Josh felt trapped by the voice in his head, but to those around him, the voice was liberating. It kept nagging Josh to pronounce to everyone that they were forgiven and to decree that they should forgive one another. The voice forced Josh to proclaim that all were required to pursue **tikkun olam**—the repair of the world—into a just society, to share **chesed**—loving kindness—with one another, and to walk with **anavah**—humility.

"I think it's really God! I think you are hearing God's actual voice," Yehud whispered excitedly to Josh each night as they lay together in bed. "The messages feel too true to be from anyone else." First Yehud, next Shimon, Andraus, then most everybody at both the job lot and the group home, everyone was excited to hear the latest proclamations from Josh's voice. His friends became followers and together, obeying the many commandments from the God voice in Josh's head, they all walked away from their jobs, homes and, for a few, even their families. It would be a new type of community, one out on the streets. It would be the Kingdom of Heaven on Earth, right here and right now.

It was fun at first, even inspiring, and Josh felt very honored to have been chosen as the messenger, but over the next several months, this honor became a horrific burden. How could he concentrate with all of these ceaseless exhortations inside his head? "Follow me." "Follow me." "Follow me." The voice was redundant and repetitive. Follow me where? When? How? The voice contradicted itself regularly and rarely gave coherent commands. It was hopeless. Josh's mood turned sour, then sad, and finally into a sort of persistent melancholy that not even Yehud could break. Josh shut down. He lost interest in preaching, in sex, in eating, even in sleeping. He had no energy for anything, and every movement of his body became slow and sluggish. Mostly, though, he was overcome by a tremendous guilt: he was failing to obey God's commands.

He was never actually suicidal—he disagreed with Dr. Fischman about this. He did not want to kill himself, but God—or at least the voice inside his head that said it was God—it *did* want him to die. God wanted him as a sacrifice. He wanted Josh to be like the lamb sacrificed at the first **Pesach**, to offer his life to spare humanity from destruction. His death would redeem man, reconciling man to God. But the reasons the voice gave for Josh dying changed daily.

The variations were often senseless and contradictory. Sometimes, his sacrifice was to bring about the salvation of all humanity, saving us from sin and its consequences, from death and separation from God. Other times, his sacrifice was to suffer in humanity's place in order to liberate humanity from sin and death. This way, God could forgive humans without punishing them while still maintaining divine justice. The idea was that God's wrath against sin was so mighty that it would destroy all of humanity, but Josh could be a substitute. He could let himself be killed in place of his fellow humans and thus save humanity from total destruction. Another time, the voice told Josh that he was supposed to offer his life in death as a sort of ransom to free humanity from its sins before God. But how was his life so "perfect" that he could swap it for the "imperfect" lives of the rest of humanity? The voice once even told Josh that he was supposed to succeed where Adam had failed. He would undo the wrong that Adam had committed when he was expelled from Eden, and—somehow?—with his blood sacrifice, lead his fellow humans on to eternal life and moral perfection. Each new reason God gave for Josh's dying generated more questions than answers.

And whatever those answers might be, by far the bigger conundrum for Josh was the *killing himself* part. **Halacha** is clear that suicide is a sin. Genesis Rabbah 34:13: We are forbidden to murder, and so each of us is similarly forbidden from "murdering" ourselves. And so this current commandment from the God voice was simply impossible to fulfill. Josh begged God daily to stop harassing him: "Please, take this suffering away from me!" He could agree to be sacrificed. That was the easy part. But trying to get himself killed so far proved impossible— it was so much more difficult than killing himself directly—that is, at least finding a way to do so without committing either the sins of murder or suicide. He could entice others to kill him, but then he would be motivating others to commit murder, also another sin. The circularity spiraled outward toward infinity.

It was on a **shabbos** morning during this darkest of times, soon after they had first formed their community, that Josh began hearing a second voice. It was softer and warmer than the first and spoke more rationally and consistently. The two voices did not get along and neither voice would shut up. They quibbled and contradicted one another as they narrated a running commentary on Josh's every thought and movement. Their babel became a tumult and, by that **motza'ei shabbat**, Josh was in a stupor.

He awoke much later that night after the rain had stopped. Yehud lay asleep beside him in their tent. His boyfriend had become so thin and dirty. They all were. None of them had eaten well in weeks. Josh was rarely hungry anymore anyway, and he had secret hopes that perhaps his recent fasting might somehow starve out the two warring voices in his head. As he lay there in his sleeping bag, he felt a sudden odd burst of actual energy, finally, and so he unzipped their tent and then slipped on his boots to wander the wet city streets before dawn. He loved the earthy smell after a rainfall, and perhaps a walk would lift his mood and ease his restlessness.

When he passed by a bakery, the smell of freshly baked bread renewed his hunger. The second voice in his head mumbled to him, "If you are God's servant, then why not use God's power to satisfy your hunger?" It enticed him. "What harm would it do to transform a few cobblestones on the street into loaves of fresh baked bread?" Josh stopped on the sidewalk near the bakery and inhaled deeply. He savored the sweet smell of the gooey dough toasting brown inside. His dry mouth slowly wet with saliva. He looked down, then kneeled and placed his hand above a stone on the walkway. He closed his eyes, concentrated, and began to recite the ***hamotzi*** blessing over bread but then stopped himself, remembering his ***anavah***, his humility. "Man does not live by bread alone," he scolded aloud, "but on every word that comes from the mouth of God." He spit the slobber from his mouth onto the stone instead. God satisfies every hunger. He smiled at this small victory, then frowned at otherwise feeling utterly defeated.

He had lost. He lost to sadness and anxiety and to the exhaustion of fighting these and other nightmares. So much noise. The voices would not shut up, first God's voice and now this other voice, too. He was hungry but fasted. He was restless but enervated. He was awake but longed for sleep. No silence. No food. No energy. No sleep. The waking world of dawn blurred for him into an incoherent dreamscape. It became hard to discern the real from the unreal.

Josh stumbled along a few blocks further, past the bakery, until he came to the old courthouse, one of the larger buildings in the center of the city. He used the last of his energy to climb the dumpster out back, then jumped onto the second-floor fire escape. From there, it was easy to climb the cold metal ladders and railings outside, one floor up to the next, and the next, until finally, he stood upon the rooftop.

The dawn light broke. Josh moved to the ledge of the roof above the front face of the courthouse. He stretched out his arms and lifted his hands above the city as if in a blessing. The street below began to bustle with commuters and street vendors.

"Jump."

A small crowd began forming on the courthouse steps many stories below.

"Jump!"

The voices down below were screaming something, but that second voice in his head yelled at him much more clearly. "Jump! Your feet will never hit the pavement. If this is all real, God's angels will catch you and carry you aloft. You need to put this all to the test."

December on 5C4

Jump. It would be such a relief. To know or to not know. Josh raised his left foot and began to step forward into the air. He stumbled, but then a gust of wind pushed him back onto the rooftop. He landed hard on his buttocks. The spanking reminded him of punishment in the ***cheder***. He laughed as he remembered his elementary school and those first basic lessons. God needs no testing. He is God. He alone quenches every thirst. Josh remembered **Massah**, the Testing, and mumbled his Deuteronomy. "**Lo tenasu et Yahweh elohim kaaser nissitem bammassah.**" He translated it aloud to the second voice in his head. "You shall not tempt Yahweh your God as you tempted him in Massah."

He sat there for seconds, maybe minutes more, then stood up and reapproached the edge of the roof, but he did not return to standing upon the ledge. He noticed then, on the left front corner of the rooftop, a large mound of gravel which had been shoveled into a small temporary mountain. Josh climbed atop the gravel mound and sat comfortably atop this highest peak. He looked down at the city below; his city, perhaps every city on Earth lay down there below him. The morning light continued its rise above the courtyard as the hue of the grass below flipped from emerald to chartreuse. The crowd there grew larger; two police cars, a fire truck, and an ambulance now parked nearby.

Josh marveled at how quickly his followers had grown. They went from so few to so many in just weeks. There was power in this. He could organize his followers. It would be the logical thing to do. They could keep growing and growing. They would soon outnumber the nonbelievers and spread their message across all the cities of the world. Josh would be their leader. The world was such a disaster, and democracies were failing everywhere. Autocracy was the future. They could use force to make everything right. Perhaps a theocracy, or better yet, a monarchy with Josh as the absolute ruler of one united global kingdom. With such might, he could bring about a new Golden Age. Josh was uncertain if he was thinking all this or if the second voice was speaking all this to him, or if both were happening at the same time. But then the second voice overtook his thoughts, "Yes. Yes." It chimed in loudly. "All this you can have. Be logical. Be reasonable. Force will work. The ends will justify the means." Josh looked down again upon the city and reimagined all the other cities of the earth there below him as well. The second voice continued, "Worship logic. Serve reason. All this you can have if you follow me."

Suddenly, Josh felt arms from behind him grapple him by his shoulders, two arms to each shoulder. "Get away. Away from me!" Josh yelled first at the officers, but then much more loudly at the second voice in his head. The policemen pulled him backward and down from the gravel pile and onto the flooring of the rooftop. Josh went limp, but they still tied his arms behind his back with a white plastic zip tie.

Josh closed his eyes shut. "Away from me!" He kept yelling, concurrently, at the cops, at the second voice in his head. "Away from me!"

He was transferred to an ambulance and given an injection into his buttocks from a large syringe with a clear liquid of some kind.

And just like that, the second voice vanished from his mind, never to be heard from again.

Josh rocked then slowly on the stretcher, mumbling, over and over, "Worship the Lord your God and serve only him," as he fell into a deep slumber. The ambulance carried him across the city for the first of his many involuntary admissions to psychiatric ward 5C4 at the county hospital.

December on 5C4

AND TODAY, FIFTEEN YEARS LATER, Josh was welcomed back now for yet another involuntary admission to ward 5C4.

He awoke on his cot as his medication-induced morning nap came to an end. He opened his eyes and lay otherwise still. His heartbeat was gentle as it whooshed blood up and across his ears. He was still a bit groggy from that new red pill, and often the medications made him dizzy. The trick was to get up gradually.

Josh sat up slowly in his bed, placed both elbows on his knees, and looked down at the palms of his two open hands. He counted on his fingers. 1-2-3…8-9-10. My tenth admission. **Mazel tov!** *I hit double digits.* Josh sighed. *What a farkakte birthday present! I'll never get out in time to reach Yehud.* He knew what the staff called him. *I'm a 'frequent flyer' who just can't seem to fly away.*

Josh had a problem. Dr. Fischman had called this problem "anosognosia," but to Josh, there was nothing "gnostic" about it. Sometimes, he was a homeless apostate, a Jew who had wandered off the **derech**, living under a freeway, an unemployed gay beggar, sad and hearing voices in his head. Other times he was a benevolent son of God, shepherding a flock of followers, chosen to sacrifice himself for the forgiveness of Humanity's sins. He could be one or the other, but seemed never able to be both.

Dr. Fischman had explained to Josh that he had other choices; in particular, he could choose to be neither. But first, Josh had to understand that he had a disease, a very treatable one, if he was willing to take his medications. But it was hard for this message to stick. Josh would understand it briefly, faintly, and parrot the idea back, but then it just sort of evaporated away from his mind.

During those first few admissions, Josh refused all medications. Over time, he learned that this just meant that they would keep him locked up longer. His 72-hour hold would be extended to a fourteen-day hold, and then they would force him to attend a capacity hearing. There was this idea called *informed consent*. If Josh refused to "consent" to take medication after being "informed" of his diagnosis and the need for medications to treat it, the hospital could take him to court to petition the state to force him to take the medications anyway. The police, paramedics, and ER doctors would give him all sorts of short-acting antipsychotic injections as "emergency medications" against his will; they did this all the time. But once locked up in the psychiatric ward itself, Josh had learned that he needed to "consent" to take further medications.

A sort of traveling mobile court would appear each Thursday in the ward common room. Benches, tables, and chairs were all hastily rearranged. There was a mental health court judge, a county counsel for the hospital, and even a public defender assigned to Josh. It was always the same. He would be rapidly tried and sentenced, then forced to take the medications anyway. Dr. Fischman would try to get a full conservatorship beyond fourteen days and would always fail. The trouble was so common as to be the norm amongst Josh's homeless brethren. Josh was too healthy to stay sick and too sick to stay healthy. His illness did make him a danger to himself during the brief crises preceding each hospital admission, but he was otherwise not regularly a danger to himself and never a danger to others, and, even in florid psychosis, he always maintained a "rational" plan for obtaining food, shelter, and clothing—and the county courts affirmed that choosing homelessness and begging for food and clothing counted as a "rational" plan for self-care. And thus, the courts had no grounds for forcing Josh into prolonged treatment.

By his fifth admission, Josh had learned he could get discharged much sooner, sometimes even in just one or two days, if he just agreed to take the medications right away.

Josh was not against the medication*s per se*—they worked. They took away the God voice in his head. It shut Him up. His cold and grumpy voice became warm and loving, then still and small, then an unintelligible susurration, then silence. At first, this made Josh happier, but then also sadder. He reveled in the quiet, content in his sudden aloneness. But then this aloneness became loneliness, as the medications cut off Josh's small soul from the grand infinite oversoul, the **Ein Sof**, the Endless One. He swiftly forgot any past annoyances and then just yearned to hear Him again, that beautiful, mellifluous, soothing God voice in his head.

And, so far, that voice had always returned. Dr. Fischman gave him thirty days of medication after each discharge from the hospital. He would even take it at first, but then Shimon or Andraus got their hands on the bottle, and they would sell it on the streets for money to give to the poor. Ms. Longhini, the social worker, finally discovered this pattern during his last admission, and so she and Dr. Fischman agreed that if Josh were to return, they would start him on a new long-acting "depot" injectable medication—one that lasted a full three months. This

December on 5C4

would finally end the God voice in his head forever. A part of Josh was dreading this. This part needed Josh to escape the ward before his birthday, before the scheduled depot injection tomorrow.

As Josh stood up from the edge of his bed, he lifted his gaze from his hands to the large round clock cemented on the wall behind his cot. 1:45PM. He had overslept through lunch—that red pill was strong. If he didn't hurry up, he'd miss Process Group entirely. Josh knew the ward schedule viscerally, having internalized it via the sheer familiarity of his many admissions over the years. He could recite it by day of the week and hour of the day. 5C4 was a psychiatric ward in an old county facility that served the uninsured and the underinsured, but they were as dutiful, diligent, and rigorous as any fancy new private hospital.

The staff and patients were kept busy: 7AM was wake-up, grooming, then breakfast; 8AM was for morning medications; 8:30AM was Community Meeting; 9AM was Goals Group; 9:30AM was for hygiene tasks (chores such as laundry and shaving); 10AM was outdoor time in the courtyard with daily stretching; 11AM was Cognitive Behavioral Therapy Group (on Mondays, Wednesdays and Fridays) and Dialectic Behavioral Therapy Group (on Tuesdays and Thursdays); 12PM was lunch; 1PM was Process Group (on Mondays through Fridays) and Journaling Group (on weekends); 2PM was indoor free time; 3PM was Discharge Planning with Relapse Prevention Group (on Mondays, Wednesdays and Fridays) or Recovery Group (on Tuesdays and Thursdays); 4PM was Occupational Therapy (mostly crafts, but music on Wednesdays, and dogs and cats visited on Fridays); 5PM was dinner; 6PM was outdoor time in the courtyard; 7PM was free time with phone calls and family visits; 8:00PM was reading and journaling time; 8:30PM was for evening medications; 9PM was bedtime with lights out. Each day of the week also had a theme: Monday was identifying patterns; Tuesday was problem formation and solving; Wednesday was power and control; Thursday was trust and respect; Friday was healthy communication; Saturday was creating change; and Sunday was healthy relationships. Over the decade and a half of Josh's visits, the hourly schedule and daily themes had never once varied.

Josh looked again at the wall clock as he exited his room. *1:45PM on a Monday. Process Group would be nearly over.* Though still a bit dizzy, he managed to shuffle his way into the common room next door.

VI

Josh entered the common room and prepared himself a cup of green tea from the bench near the door. All the tables had been folded and stacked to the side wall to be replaced by a ring of thirteen chairs arranged in a circle in the center. Josh sat down in one of the empty seats.

He was unfamiliar with the therapist running the group—the guy must be new—and he certainly was young, maybe younger than even Josh himself. He was a thin white man with blue eyes and blond hair. He had a well-trimmed goatee, and his long hair was pulled back into a ponytail, tied with a brown elastic and a long eagle feather. He wore a blue scrub shirt and denim jeans. Around his neck was a sterling silver chain with a large turquoise stone embedded in the center. The shirt pocket on his scrub top had a name tag clipped to it. There were three printed lines, the first in black bold, "Oscar R. Cody, Psy. D.", the second in red italics "call me Roy", and the third in smaller type, "(he/him/his)".

Roy passed the talking stick to a heavy patient in distinctive red pajamas. It was Nick from this morning. This therapist may have been new, but that talking stick had been used here in Process Group for as long as anyone could remember. It was a traditional tribal speaker's staff—about two feet in length, a dark hard brown wood, carved with a pattern of shells, also an eagle, a bear, and a wolf, and then some black bird feathers tied to a hole on each end with a suede cord. In Process Group, custom dictated that the talking stick be passed from patient to patient with only the person holding it being allowed to speak.

Nick began. "So why am I here? I'll tell you why I am here—because no good deed goes unpunished. Especially three of them. I could pretend not to remember, but I remember everything." Nick scanned the group as he talked, he smiled sheepishly toward everyone, then nodded his head in greeting when he met Josh's gaze. "When the firemen found me, I had been stuck in that chimney for over six hours. It was a lot of time to think and more than enough to start crashing too."

Josh noted how markedly different Nick seemed now from their argument hours ago at breakfast. His speech was slower, softer, clearer. Nick sat steadily and sincerely, with no anger, radiating only resolve and serenity. His arms rested comfortably atop his folded knees, neither tapping nor fidgeting. He appeared so much calmer to Josh now from this morning as to be nearly unrecognizable. Those new red pills must be miraculous.

Nick rolled the talking stick between both hands as he continued. "How did I get stuck in a chimney of all places? Well, first, I climbed up a large cypress tree growing next to the chimney of their old house, and then I pushed off the chimney cap. It slid off easily enough. I peered over, used a flashlight to peer down the flue, then dropped the bag of gold coins. It fell, but my aim was off, and the bag got stuck just above the damper on the smoke chamber. So, it didn't make it down into the fireplace itself. But I was committed—several lines of coke with no sleep committed. Look, I know I'm heavy—ever since my wife Jessica had me quit smoking my pipe, my weight ballooned up past three hundred pounds, but I was a serious athlete in my younger days—I even played college ball—anyway, so I dove boots first right into the chimney. I squiggled and squirmed my way down the flue like an inchworm. At the bottom, above the smoke chamber, I kicked the bag of gold coins with my boots and pushed them off the damper flap and into the fireplace below. I then just reversed it all; I squirmed then squiggled, making my way up the flue instead of down. Of course, it was all so much harder, going against gravity and with no handholds or footholds to speak of. I did it, though. Maybe thirty minutes later, I even made it past the roofline. But I was so exhausted, then my waist and my belly… it all just got stuck *right there*. My head, arms, and upper body were outside the chimney top, but my belly, butt, and legs were all trapped beneath."

Nick gazed out the windows at the snow flurries falling outside. "You know, I had never even heard of cocaine until last year. But I had to go to so many meetings with so many bankers before we could take the company public. I'm the CEO of Myra Toys. I didn't earn the role so much as inherit it after my uncle died two years ago. He founded the company with my dad; they named it after our hometown from before we emigrated.

"Well, becoming CEO was not an easy transition for me, and there was no time to grieve." Nick lowered his head and closed his eyes. He spoke softly, softly for Nick, "Too many people have died on me over the years, too many to remember." He sniffled for a moment but then tapped his forehead with the end of the talking stick.

The fat man lifted his head, opened his eyes, and continued again, rapidly, "My uncle had died right before the beginning of our IPO. And so I jumped in to head both the IPO and our expansion from our main production facility way up north. We now have a worldwide distribution with a facility on every continent.

You wouldn't think it, but the toy business is beyond cutthroat—you've got to have factories and distribution centers with real-time warehouse management systems down to the millisecond. It's not just about massive production, but also rapid delivery with integration between your warehouse and transportation systems to optimize consolidation and utilization." Nick briefly placed the stick on his lap and made air quotes with his fingers. "Kids these days want *new* toys, and they want them *now*. It's like everyone wants tomorrow's toys yesterday. This business now is nothing like the small wooden toy store my dad and uncle first started. It's all today like some sort of fairytale gone horribly wrong."

Nick coughed, then continued, staring at no one in particular down and into the center of the circle of chairs. "So last year, I was sitting on a truly unimaginable pile of cash. The cocaine was—and really always has been—just a small expense. It kept my mind sharp and alert and helped me not sleep when my job demanded it, which it often did. After last year's IPO windfall, on a typical work night, me and the c-suite gang would blow through a line or two then head over to the old hotel on 34th Street to relax with the escorts there. That's really where all my troubles began."

Nick gripped each end of the talking stick with his hands. "I mean, they call themselves escorts, but let's be honest, they're prostitutes. Whores really. The bartender, Omar, is basically a pimp for us fancy guys. The girls don't speak much English, and they try not to teach them, but what Omar didn't know is that I speak fluent Turkish. You see, I was born in Arsinoe, lived in Myra as a kid and then, after we immigrated over here, my family kept speaking Turkish at home when I was growing up. We johns are not supposed to know it, but I discovered that Omar's girls aren't really smuggled over, so much as trafficked. They tell the girls they are signing them up for cleaning or restaurant jobs, then when they get here they are forced to turn tricks until they pay off their smuggling debt. But also, they pretty much get as many of them hooked on heroin as they can, and then the girls just can never pay off any of their debts at all.

"I wasn't supposed to know any of this stuff. But there was something about Alara—my regular girl—she was incredible at her job. I won't pretend that I loved her or that she had any romantic emotions for me, 'cause you know, it's business, it's like a hairdresser or a masseuse or any other service industry type job—you both keep it professional, but you also become friendly if you work together regularly. Alara was young, only eighteen, and could easily have been my daughter's age if my wife and I were able to have kids. Her English was poor and then I surprised her one day by talking with her in Turkish. She told me everything. How her father had been a wealthy merchant in Turkey before the war. How he lost everything and used what little remained of his money to smuggle over himself, Alara, and her two younger sisters here. How Omar and his gang were forcing her and her two younger sisters to *work* to pay off their remaining smuggling debt. The youngest sister is only fourteen, I mean, that's sick, right? They also kept trying to get Alara and her sisters to shoot up."

Nick paused and looked up at the therapist. "Roy, everything here is confidential, right? Basically, it all stays in group?"

"Yes, Nick, this is just for you; for you to help yourself by sharing your story. What is shared in group stays in group."

Nick looked back down and continued, "Her story stuck with me. It haunted me. Their dad is just old and sick, bedridden at this point. So, I managed to get Alara to give me her home address. If I gave her cash, it would bring too many questions, plus frankly, I'd have to pay heavy gift taxes, and it'd all be traceable. I needed a way to give Alara and her sisters money that was confidential and untraceable, also discrete, so I could avoid pissing off Omar and his group. Those guys don't fuck around. I first withdrew 100K in gold coins from the bank in a money sack, about four pounds of gold, enough to pay off the baby sister Zehra's debt—the fourteen-year-old—and some more for living expenses and college tuition. I drove by one night and just threw the bag in an open window at their house. Alara let me know when they got it. The next night, I did the same thing for Fatma, the sixteen-year-old. Finally, last night, I came by, ready to throw a final bag of gold coins through the window—this one for Alara herself—but somebody, probably their dad, locked the windows. That's when I got the idea to climb up the side of the house and throw it down the chimney. Not my finest inspiration, but I was pretty coked up at the time."

Nick stopped, then laughed. "Ho, ho, ho. Ha, ha, ha." It was his usual deep belly laugh. "And twelve hours later, here I am."

His timing was nearly perfect. Nick looked up at the clock face on the upper wall above the common room window. Nearly 2PM with one minute to go precisely.

He reached toward Roy to give him back the talking stick. "Hey everyone, why do elves make such great listeners?"

He paused for comic effect. "Nobody? Because they're all ears!" Nick released the stick, then laughed a final time: "Ho, ho ho. Ha, ha, ha."

Josh laughed too.

Nobody else seemed to think it was funny.

VII

AT 2PM, a two-tone preamble trumpeted aloud through the ward PA system. A young woman's voice then announced, "It's time for Free Time. Let's play games and have some fun."

Everyone—the patients, the new therapist Roy, and the various orderlies—stood and worked together to unfold the furniture and rearrange the room back into various round tables with chairs.

"I'm so sorry for this morning," Nick approached Josh and gently placed an arm on his shoulder. "I was still pretty coked up. I barely remember what we argued about, I just remember being angry at everything and everyone, but mostly at myself." He sighed and shook his head. "You were just an easy target." Nick's eyes were glossy. "Can you forgive me?"

Josh listened inside for the God voice. His medication from this morning had muffled it, but he still could make out some mumblings. Josh spoke aloud the message. "Forgive others and you will be forgiven." Then Josh folded both his hands over his heart and turned directly toward Nick. "I forgive you." He slapped his chest, "Seven times. Seventy times seven times. And beyond. I forgive you." Josh bowed his head, "Will you forgive me?"

"Thank you!" Nick had begun crying. "And, of course, I forgive you too." He blew his nose, then dried his eyes, both times using the red sleeves of his hospital pajamas. "Though you didn't do anything that needs forgiving. I was the asshole."

The two partnered to roll out a flattened round table from the vertical stack near the sidewall. Josh opened the bottom legs and Nick the top ones. Together they lifted from opposite sides and flipped the table up and over onto its feet.

Nick raised an index finger to Josh, gesturing for him to wait. He turned, grabbed two chairs, turned back, then asked, "*Viln tsu spiln damkes?*"

Josh replied affirmatively, "*Akei.*" He grabbed the checkerboard and the box of checkers from the shelf behind him, then stopped himself suddenly, "Hey Nick, how do you know Yiddish?"

December on 5C4

"I don't really. I speak English and my native Turkish, but I know a bit of every language." Nick sat down in the chair and pushed himself in, resting his elbows on the table. "Well, not every one—there are over 6,500—but I probably know a bit of the hundred most common."

Josh sat opposite Nick, blew the dust off the checkerboard, and placed it down between them. It was old, perhaps even older than the hospital itself. Josh noted that the board was made entirely from walnut. The craftsman had interlocked sapwood with heartwood to create a patterning of light and dark squares. The sapwood squares were stained to a creamy white, while the heartwood squares were tinted to enhance their more subtle dark green hue.

"Before I became CEO, I was COO, and Myra Inc. sent me on trips everywhere for years. I basically lived my life out of a big red sack. I must have carried that bag over my shoulder forever. I don't know how my wife put up with it." Nick opened up the checker box, which was also made from walnut.

Nick stared down into the square box and continued. "The world is such an enormous, bright place, filled with different peoples and cultures, but in my travels, I have found that our similarities far eclipse our differences. Myra Inc. is just like any other corporation now: transnational, international, multinational. Nothing is just *national* anymore. Countries divide us, but corporations unite us. Capitalism knows no borders." Nick arced his right hand above the table in emphasis. "Sometimes, I even flew all over the globe and back again in just a single night!"

Josh considered how little he himself had traveled. He had never really traveled at all—so much as lived in different places—just four actually, all nearby to one another, and all—until the last—in an insular religious community. There was Bayt Lahm, where he was born, then Kemet, briefly as a toddler, then Natsrat, where he grew up, and then this city right here. Of course, he had visited the city as a child, but these last many years, ever since he had wandered off the **derech**, the city had become his new home. He agreed with Nick from this morning that he and his followers were technically houseless, but this city, especially Godsmane Park and the old Oil Press Neighborhood, this city nevertheless was their home too.

"There are basically three groups of phrases you need to learn in any language, and then you can get by almost anywhere you're traveling." Nick lifted his right hand again to begin to count with his fingers. "The first is how to say 'Please' and 'Thank you.' That's just courtesy and will get you a long way. The second is how to ask for a beer and how to ask where the bathroom is. These two phrases take care of your nutritional, biological, and social needs—suddenly, you are fun in another language. Finally, the third is how to ask, 'What is this?' With this one little phrase, you can point at anything and slowly learn the language wherever you are." Nick clapped his hands together. "So, at that point, you can say please and thank you, drink a beer, take a piss, and sit in a bar pointing at things to learn more of the language. My hosts invariably found me highly entertaining." Nick smiled and winked. "And being charming is fundamental to making deals." He placed an index finger on the side of his nose and nodded. "But really, I found that most people I met spoke a little English, and so whenever I made an effort, they'd make an effort back and so speak English to me if they knew it."

It stopped snowing outside the window. Other tables in the common room were abuzz with games and activities. At one, several patients were spinning tops and exchanging fake gold coins. At another, three were drumming on small bongos, each beaded with red, black, and green triangular netting. Nearby, two others played backgammon. There was also an art project with colored powders and sands. The staff even lit a few candelabras and placed them on the windowsills.

Josh and Nick reached into the checker box and grabbed the pieces. Josh admired how the two opposing sets of round pieces were made from a light cream boxwood versus a deep rose bloodwood. The cut, finish, and weight of the pieces were perfect. This was fine craftsmanship. Nick chose the bloodwood, leaving Josh with the boxwood.

They set their checkers on the board. Nick then placed one of each checker type into each hand, making fists to hide them. He swirled his fists around one another. "You choose".

Josh tapped a fist, and Nick opened it to reveal a light cream checker. "You go first." He quickly closed the same hand into a fist and reopened it. "Or do you?" The checker had become a deep rose color.

Josh raised his eyebrows and opened his mouth.

"Ho, ho, ho! Ha, ha, ha!" Nick was certainly calmer since the morning but still had his distinctive deep belly laugh. "I learned this trick from my good friend Winter, he's a professional, but I'm pretty good myself." He closed his fist again and reopened it to reveal the original light cream checker. "Magic is all in the wrists. At least mine." He reached over to return Josh's checker. "You go first."

The two played several games, at first slowly, then rapidly. The slow clink of the checkers evolved into a steady staccato tapping. They had wildly different strategies, but nevertheless, their games kept ending in a tie—sometimes with forty-move draws, other times with three position repetitions. Nick typically managed to crown just one piece as a king and kept the rest of his men uncrowned. His strategy was more aggressive, the one king directing out its smaller minions—

which he kept calling "elves"—to do its bidding across the board. Josh's strategy was peaceful, committed to nonviolence, avoiding conflict—and thus captures—whenever possible. He initially sacrificed pieces left and right but somehow managed to crown all his surviving pieces into kings.

Conversation flowed above as checkers parried below.

"So, Josh," Nick's blue eyes met Josh's brown. "You know why I'm here from my story in group." Their hands continued to slide and jump the checkers. "Why are you here? I mean *really*."

Josh shook his head but held his gaze. "I don't want to be here."

"Why not?" Nick paused the game on his turn to lift his hands and point about the room. "I mean, you've got a roof, food, heat, a bathroom, a shower. This has got to be better than a leaky tent near a freeway." They were both briefly silent. Nick completed his turn, and the game played through quickly to another draw. Then they reset their pieces. "Don't let perfection be the enemy of the good or the good enough."

"That's exactly the problem. Perfection." Josh moved his pieces first this round. "I've seen it, heard it, smelled, tasted, and even touched it. I've been immersed in it, yet somehow not immolated by it. My soul has met what my people call the Oversoul." The clink of the checkers accelerated. Josh paused his move and sighed. "You see, for the last sixteen years, the voice of God has been speaking to me."

Josh and Nick both now stopped their game as Josh continued. "Perfection is the enemy of the good, but for me, I've met perfection. And perfection has met me and just won't leave me alone. I hear His voice. God's voice. After that, how can there be enemies anymore? Or allies even? We are all friends and family. Everyone is my neighbor, and the voice commands me to love everyone as I love myself."

Nick lowered his shoulders and stroked his beard. He asked Josh quietly, *very quietly* for Nick, "What does the voice sound like?"

"It's not like a regular sound. It doesn't come from any one direction. The words surround me and soak into my head, then I hear them." Josh circled his hands around his head for emphasis. "When it started, it was a magnificent experience—the voice was loving and calming, gentle and sweet. He would come and go. But then, one day, He came but refused to leave. His voice became harsher and colder, and he wouldn't stop commenting on everything I did, every day, all day.

"He's bossy, too." Josh picked up one of his lighter whitish checkers and held it between his fingers. "What the voice commands of other people seems relatively easy—He wants us to forgive one another and to work together to seek justice, love kindness, and be humble. My followers love this part." Josh put down the white checker and exchanged it for a darker, redder piece. He lifted it up. "But what the voice commands of *me* is impossible. I feel so hopeless because I can't obey God's commandment, then I feel *so* guilty and *so* sad, then everything just sort of shuts down. It's *tsuris* beyond anything imaginable. I want to sleep but can't; I get restless but have no energy; I get hungry but can't eat. I usually get hospitalized after that."

Josh held the red piece over the checker box and dropped it in. "It's confusing, but God wants me as a sacrifice. Somehow, my death is supposed to redeem all of humanity. But killing myself or making others kill me… both are forbidden. I know it sounds ridiculous, but He says that I am not supposed to live much past thirty-three, and tomorrow I actually turn thirty-three. I had a huge fight with my boyfriend, and I need to see him. I want us to make up before it's too late."

He looked down at the table and dropped the errant white piece into the checker box. "But there's more. After my last admission, Ms. Longhini and Dr. Fischman made a plan to inject me with a new long-acting version of my medicine." He gazed up again and met Nick's eyes. "You see, after this injection tomorrow morning, I won't hear the God voice again. The injection lasts for three months, and even before that, Ms. Longhini will come with the Outreach team and just re-inject me. It'll end. I'll never hear the God voice again after tomorrow." Josh closed the lid of the checker box and shook the two checkers inside. "His voice is beyond the most beautiful thing you can imagine. I don't want to fail in God's mission for me, though I don't know quite how to succeed."

"Ho, ho, ho! Ha, ha, ha!" Nick guffawed with one of his deep laughs. "Why succeeding is easy, Josh. It's like I told my old friend Winter. You've just gotta place one foot in front of the other." Nick grabbed two checkers, too, one white in one hand, one red in the other. He held the checkers between his middle and index fingers, locked his two thumbs, and then pantomimed his hands into a pretend man walking across the table with shoes made of the checkers. "Place one foot in front of the other, and soon enough, you'll be walking across the floor." He stopped his pretend man from walking at the edge of the table, then folded his hands together and pointed both index fingers out toward two large, locked, bright red double doors. These were just outside the other side of the common room, past the nursing station. "Soon enough, you'll be walking out *those* doors."

Josh frowned. "I don't expect you to believe me. Though I'm always surprised by how many people do, some even follow me. I don't understand it. But it doesn't matter anyway. The God voice says that beliefs don't make any of us better people, it's our behaviors that do."

December on 5C4

Nick turned ashen. He placed both palms on the table and leaned in low toward Josh. He whispered, "I'm sorry. I meant to be silly, not cynical. Sincerely. I'm just so happy right now. You've made me so happy." He lifted his shoulders, kept his palms down on the table, and returned to a normal volume. "Because I do. I do believe you, Josh." He held his gaze with Josh, lifting his eyebrows in earnest. "After our argument this morning, after you asked if you could pray for me, it's weird, but I heard you somehow speaking the words even though I was all the way over in my room by then. You prayed in Hebrew, and yet I could understand every word you spoke."

Nick pointed at his ear. "It was odd at the time. I didn't think much of it; I guess I didn't think it was real. After all, I was still amped up from all the coke." He lowered his voice and leaned in towards Josh. "But then, after they gave me the red pill and brought me back to my room, something happened. It was like a warm feeling all over my body and mind, I fell into a brief but deep sleep." He tilted his head and closed his eyes, "Sort of a super nap." then opened them. "When I awoke, I was better—all better. And I mean *all*. My mind was rested. No more grief. I cried, I finally cried, something so simple, yet so hard for someone like me. No more anger. No more racing thoughts. My cravings for cocaine vanished. I don't need it, and I don't want it ever again. But not just that. The hearing in my left ear is *normal* again. That cataract in my right eye is gone. Even the old scar on my right knee has vanished. One might think, 'Wow, that must have been one hell of a red pill,' but you see…" Nick lifted both hands in front of Josh and rolled them about, pushing his right hand forward in a fist. He turned it over, then slowly unfolded the fingers. A red pill sat in his palm. "I never took the red pill."

Nick reached forward with his left hand over the checkerboard and grabbed Josh's fingers. "I pretended. I drank the water in the paper cup but just palmed the pill." He squeezed Josh's hand, then let go. "It was you, Josh. I never took their medicine. It was your prayer, Josh. You healed me."

Nick's eyes became watery. "Josh, you really hear Him, don't you?"

Josh smiled and nodded. His reality was always such a revelation to the others around him. He recited Rabbi Nachman's famous prayer. "**Adonai shalom, berachnu b'shalom**. God who is peace, bless us in peace." He grabbed Nick's hands with his own and folded their fingers together. "Nick, peace be unto you."

Nick teared, slowly, then steadily, into a rhythmic sobbing as he lowered his head and closed his eyes.

Josh closed his eyes, too. He tried to summon the God voice. It was muffled under the medication from this morning, but Josh could still hear His whispers. He repeated the words outward, "God says to tell you that 'you have seen me and you have believed. Imagine the blessings out there for everyone that will never see me and yet still believe.'"

Just then, a distant rumble echoed in the sky outside. An odd flash of bright light came through the windows, just for a moment, then pervaded the room. There was a puff of ozone as the electricity in the unit flickered on and off. Then nothing more.

"I'm sorry. I'm so sorry for ever doubting you." Nick rubbed his tears dry with the cuff of his pajama sleeve. "Please let me make it up to you. Please let me help you." He lowered his voice—as best he could—to his nearest approximation of a whisper, "We've got to get you out of here before tomorrow. It's your birthday. It's my busiest workday. You need to be freed, and I want to be free. Let's try for tonight."

Nick and Josh turned silent as they returned the checkers to the box.

Nick looked at the clock high up on the wall. "I have to go meet with the therapist one-on-one next, so let's meet up later at dinner. We can make a plan then."

An unusually short nursing assistant dressed in a red shirt with green pants came to their table and motioned for Nick to follow her.

Nick stood, walked with her, then turned back towards Josh. "Oh, and hey, Josh—do you know why elves go to therapy?"

Josh shrugged his shoulders.

"To help with their *elf-esteem*! Ho, ho, ho! Ha, ha, ha!"

December on 5C4

VIII

JOSH CHUCKLED AT NICK'S JOKE as he sat alone at the table after Nick's departure. *What a strange man. And what is it about his fixation with elves? Can he really help me escape?* Josh had never considered the possibility of simply escaping 5C4, to stop the cycle, to just leave the story—his chronicles, this myth—behind. Should he? Could he? If he left that night, then he would avoid tomorrow's injection entirely. The pill would wear off, and he could hear God's full voice again. It was all so confusing; how could a part of him want something and still another part of him not want that same thing, yet both so badly and both at the same time?

When the clock on the common room wall turned to 3PM, an unusually musical four-tone tune played over the ward speakers. Three short G's followed by one long F. A male voice then announced in monotone: "Discharge planning in the common room. All patients, please report for discharge planning in the common room."

The new therapist, Roy, entered the room. He pushed a few tables toward the walls and rearranged the chairs again into one large circle. He placed his clipboard on one seat, then pushed it back a bit from the ring of chairs. He went to the wall and unfolded a much heavier and older folding chair, one with dark mahogany legs and a velvet purple cushion. He then slid it in front of his much simpler, newer folding seat.

Josh stood up, moved over, and sat down again on one of the regular chairs in the circle. Other patients began ambling in and sat down in the circle as well. Roy sat down behind the larger wooden chair and then reviewed his clipboard.

"Eh-hem," a woman cleared her throat at the entrance to the room.

Roy stood, and the various other patients rose as well.

Ms. Longhini entered the room and marched to the large wooden chair. The thin woman walked with a military, almost regal, bearing. She wore tight camouflage army pants with brown boots laced taut. Her shirt was a dark green scrub top with no sleeves. Her tan arms were noticeably muscled and toned, particularly for an older lady. She had black hair cut short and kept a wisp of a mustache upon her upper lip. Her eyes were black, and her irises enlarged comically through a pair of exceedingly thick glasses she wore banded across her head. She sat down in her wooden cushioned chair, then Roy sat, then everyone else.

"Welcome all. We will discuss discharge planning in general as a group, then we'll break off for briefer small group meetings between yourselves and Dr. Cody and me." Ms. Longhini spoke at a regular volume but with a firmness that bordered on yelling. "Discharge planning is the first and primary task of any hospitalization, for any reason. It is much more important than the individual treatments you each may receive during your hospital stays. Without discharge planning, our hospital would fill up with patients, and then we'd be too crowded to offer any treatments at all. Also, the county requires indigent patients to be discharged before they pay their bills, and so without discharge planning, the flow of money would cease. And without money, we cannot offer effective treatment to any of you."

Josh had heard this lecture many times before. As most of the patients on 5C4 were typically homeless, Ms. Longhini finished her general speech but then also added in her familiar lecture on the hospital's specific legal requirements for the discharge of homeless persons: (1) Each patient's identity must be verified and recorded in a tracking log, (2) Efforts must be made to track down any next of kin, (3) Weather-appropriate clothing must be provided, (4) A final meal is given upon discharge, (5) Everyone is given a thirty day supply of all medications, or a prescription for such, (6) A list of local shelter options will be distributed, (7) Everyone will receive a discharge report written at a fifth-grade reading level, and (8) Transportation will be arranged for up to either thirty minutes or thirty miles away, but only to a fixed legal address.

Hospital discharge programs were notoriously inconsistent, but the county hospital was lucky to have not just one but two fully mobile outreach units. These were essentially well-equipped vans staffed by nurses and social workers. Ms. Longhini often drove one of the vans herself, and she would arrive twice a month to visit Josh and his followers in their tent compound beneath the freeway. In the past, she would check in with Josh, give him bottles of his medication, and urge him to take it. He had his freedom, and it was his choice to take the medicine or not. But now, the plan was for Ms. Longhini to check in with Josh at three-month intervals and inject him with medication right then and there at the park.

"I will be doing my job, and after tomorrow morning, my job will be to make sure we pierce your side with this needle every three months." Ms. Longhini showed Josh a sample injection needle. She and Josh were meeting briefly now, one-on-one, to discuss his specific discharge plans.

"The syringe will be filled with a fluid, of course, but it's basically the same thing as the chemical in your pill medicine. It's combined with an inactive part that lets it dissolve in oil, and this makes it all injectable. When shot into a muscle, it creates a store or *depot* of medication, which is released slowly over time into your system. That's why it's called a *depot injection*." Ms. Longhini snapped her fingers toward Roy, who gave her his wooden clipboard and several long metal pens.

Ms. Longhini placed the wooden clipboard on Josh's lap. She moved the palms of his hands to either side of the board. A medication consent form was affixed to the center. "It is such exciting news to finally have this in a three-month-long formulation for you. You'll get twelve full weeks of coverage per injection!" The form was already filled out completely and dated, and just needing signatures. "It solves the problem of needing to take a pill every day. If your meds get stolen or sold, or you lose them—it won't matter anymore. All you need is this depot injection four times a year, and you'll be completely covered. It guarantees perfect medication adherence, consistency, and compliance."

She reached out with her hand and placed it over Josh's forearm. "Rabbi, you'll never have to hear that voice again." Ms. Longhini always addressed Josh formally as Rabbi. "So now that we've reviewed your medication—" she squeezed his arm twice rapidly, "Do you have any last questions?"

Josh was silent. To be a Jew is to have questions, and right now, he had too many questions and too few words to ask them. The medicine made his thoughts cloudy and his voice sluggish. He closed his eyes and listened deeply for the God voice. He asked it a familiar question. *My God, my God, have you forsaken me?* No answer. Not even a whisper or a murmur arose above the muffle of his medication. *Why?*

"You just need to sign right here on this consent form." Ms. Longhini took a long metal pen and stabbed it through the curled fingers of Josh's right hand atop the wooden clipboard. "Let me help you." She placed her hand over his and moved his hand to sign his signature for him. She produced his thick cursive writing in a dark red ink.

Father, into your hands, I commend my spirit. Josh closed his eyes, searched inward again, and entreated as best he could to the God voice in his head. He had no energy to speak, but enough to pray, and always enough to forgive. *Father, please forgive them, for they do not know what they are doing.*

Ms. Longhini signed her own signature as a witness on a line across from Josh's on the form.

Josh opened his eyes and scanned the form. *It is finished. Well, almost.* He looked up at Roy and remembered his Talmud. He managed to ask, softly and gently, "Roy, could you sign as well? Per tractate *Bava Batra* a document like this should have the signature of two witnesses." He then added, in a mumbled whisper, "Also please remember that a **mahak** is **pasul**. You can't scribble. It needs to be a legible signature."

Roy turned to Ms. Longhini, who shrugged and gave him one of the long metal pens. He reached down and added his own red signature beneath Ms. Longhini's, placing a date on its side.

Josh scanned the form again. *It is finished.* He was suddenly very, very thirsty.

Ms. Longhini and Roy moved on to the next patient in line for a discharge meeting with them.

Josh arose and walked toward the large snack bench in the common room. He could feel his medication wearing off. He could use a drink—wine, grape juice even—but lemonade would have to do. He picked up a box of warm lemonade and pushed a small straw into the top.

He held the lemonade in his right hand and slowly recited a first **bracha. Baruch atah A-donay, Elo-heinu Melech Ha'Olam shehakol nihiyah bed'varo.** *Blessed are You, Lord our God, King of the universe, by Whose word all things came to be.*

He sipped the lemonade quickly. It smelled of lemon, and it tasted both sweet and sour. He found this combination lively and refreshing, oddly satisfying. His energy was returning. As he sat there, drinking and musing, a silly riddle bubbled up from his thoughts.

"What do you say to a sad elf?" Josh asked aloud to no one in particular. He waited, sipped some more lemonade, then waited some more. "Don't *be little* yourself." There was no one nearby to hear the punchline. He smiled, chuckled, then finished his drink.

He tossed the empty box into the garbage bin and then quickly recited the after-**bracha. Baruch atah Adonai Elohenu, Melekh Ha'olam borei nefashot rabot v'chesronan al kol ma she'barata l'hachayot bahem nefesh kol chai baruch chei ha'olamim.** *Blessed are You, Lord our God, King of the universe, Creator of numerous living beings and their needs, for all the things You have created with which to sustain the soul of every living being. Blessed is He who is the Life of the world.*

December on 5C4

IX

J OSH SAT ALONE at the table for a brief while before hearing the deep rumble of a male voice repeating syllables he could not understand. *"Nagsisimula na ang OT. Mga katulong mangyaring pumunta."* He looked up at the PA speaker box on the ceiling, the red light was lit, and he suspected the sound came from the box. *"Nagsisimula na ang OT. Mga katulong mangyaring pumunta."* He listened again and made out the English initials "O.T.". *"Nagsisimula na ang OT. Mga katulong mangyaring pumunta."* He looked just below the speaker box where the wall clock read 4PM. It was indeed time for Occupational Therapy to begin.

Occupational Therapy, "O.T." for short, is a form of group therapy that encourages rehabilitation through the performance and practice of ordinary activities from daily life. For patients recovering from mental illness, this typically means sharing supervised leisure activities such as games, art, or music. The specific substance of the hour varied widely over Josh's many admissions, but even at his illest, he invariably found the activities the most interesting part of most days in the unit.

Nick entered the room, pushing a large cart. This OT cart was painted red over old metal shelving, all on wheels, it was long and tall with three tiers—each level shorter than the next, and each stacked one upon the other like a birthday cake. The racks were filled with innumerable classic toys and games, though more so overflowing with the chaos of colorful art supplies: paper, cardboard, markers, crayons, pens, pencils, tape, rubber bands, popsicle sticks, glue, paint, brushes, and more.

Nick was wearing a lush red velvet robe with white trim and a matching triangular hat with a white pom-pom at the tip. He pushed the cart from behind, clenching two guide handles, as the cart seemingly floated across the common room floor.

In front of the cart were two rows of four nursing assistants pulling the load with two separate guide ropes tied to the middle shelf. They wore red scrub shirts and green pajama pants with matching triangular hats, but unlike Nick's pom-pom, their hats were tipped with bells. Each of these aides was very short, none was taller than four feet in height. They were uniformly slim with dark yellowish-brown skin. Their hair was short, straight, jet black, and spiky, and their brown eyes were almond shaped with double lidded folds. None of them had any facial hair and there was something odd about their ears... but then Josh noticed a ninth nursing aide in front between the rows, leading the others and holding a lit flashlight. He was even shorter, seemed younger, and had a flare of rosacea, making his nose remarkably red.

The cart spiraled around the room before landing in the center. Immediately, the aides quietly distributed art supplies to the various tables. Patients funneled into the room and sat around the tables. There was nearly one aide per patient today.

No words were spoken, but instrumental music seemed to come from everywhere—orchestral, with the oboe leading the melody alongside clarinet, violin, viola, bells, and chimes. The tunes were a blend of trills, grace notes, *appoggiaturas*, pedal notes, mordents, slides, and cadences. Josh tried but could not find the source of the music; when he looked up at the PA box, the red speaker light remained unlit.

The sounds, the sight - it was all so amazing! Josh's mouth opened wide; he laughed and smiled and then responded with an instinctive and joyful **shehecheyanu**. "**Baruch atah Adonai Elohenu, melekh ha'olam, shehecheyanu vekiymanu vehigi'anu lazman hazeh.**" *Blessed are You, Lord, our God, King of the Universe, who has granted us life, sustained us, and enabled us to reach this occasion.*

Nick left the cart last, after the aides, taking a large bin of art supplies and sitting beside Josh. One of the short aides moved across from them on the table and unloaded a large pile of popsicle sticks and other art supplies.

"Well, never say I don't know how to make an entrance." Nick turned toward Josh, held eye contact, and conversed freely, all while his hands grabbed popsicle sticks, rubber bands, and other art supplies, building small creations with an alacrity that Josh found astonishing. Nick's hands clenched several popsicle sticks, pipe cleaners, rubber bands, buttons, and magic markers, twisted them all together, and suddenly an appealing toy car sat on the table.

"Quite an entrance indeed, Nick." Josh was still amazed. He still heard that music everywhere, though it soon faded and stopped. "How did you get to drive the sleigh?"

"I guess it just sort of happened." Nick rolled back the toy car to prime it, then he released it, and the rubber band engine propelled it forward. "There I was, in Roy's office doing therapy, banging on drums, talking about my mother—

you know, the usual— then we ended our session, and I opened the door to leave only to see the side of the OT cart wedged tight against the exit. The cart was stuck in the hallway, trapping us in his office."

Nick reached into the pile of mixed craft supplies and continued building. "I don't speak their language very well, but I did hear them repeating the word *gulong*, which means wheel. So, I bent down, reached under the cart, and felt around. I found four wheels, one on each corner, each spinning freely, but in the center was a larger fifth wheel, rusted stuck." Nick lined up two rows of six toy soldiers each, newly made mostly from popsicle sticks, each with fully articulated joints in the arms and the legs. "I was able to use the last of my friend Winter's magic, his prestidigitation training, and so my fingers were just able to unscrew the nuts from the bolts above this wheel casing. And so, after a bit of effort, I actually detached this fifth wheel and chucked it. Who needs a fifth wheel anyway? After that, the carriage moved smoothly—it practically flew down the hall. It was *mabuhays* all around!" Nick's fingers stormed around a ball of felt and glue, then released to reveal a fluffy baby doll. "The little fellas were really appreciative, and so they let me drive the cart here from behind. It was kind of like an indoor sleigh ride."

The aide across the table from Nick and Josh grabbed the baby doll, squeezed it, and an impressive "ma-ma" squeaked out. Josh smiled, laughed, then closed his eyes and took in a slow, deep, easy breath. He could smell OT everywhere around him—from the mellow scent of glue paste to the acrid stench of rubber cement and all the aromas in between: glue dots, scotch tape, magic markers, and various gel paints.

Josh opened his eyes and watched as the short assistant busily completed crafts almost as quickly as Nick. He—or was it she? Josh couldn't tell—were they using not just their tiny hands but also a small set of files, blunt scissors, and little hammers to shape popsicle sticks, cork, pipe cleaners, paper, and more into every shape imaginable? The aide produced one toy after another after another. They did pause, however, long enough to point at Josh, and then motion to the large pile of art supplies and then to the toys on the table.

"I love working with my hands. This is so fun. It reminds me of my childhood, when Myra Toys was first starting out as just a small homemade wooden toy shop." Nick rotated his head from Josh to the short aide at their table. "*Higit pa, mangyaring.*" The aide refilled the large pile of art supplies, pushed it toward Nick, then dumped a smaller pile of supplies separately next to Josh.

Josh used yarn to slowly tie several double stacks of popsicle sticks as crosspieces to one another. He balanced his small creations on their bases and lined them up three across, a short line of little letter Ts on the tabletop. A beam of sunlight came in from the window and lit up the center T in a white glow. Josh grabbed more supplies to build a second project. "But Nick, how did you ever manage to get the red robe and the hat?"

"I already had it on. Someone brought it by this morning when I was asleep and Roy had it for me in his office during our therapy session." Nick's hands folded and ripped at a stack of red construction paper with scotch tape. "It's an old robe with a matching hat to keep me warm and cozy. Jessica sewed it for me herself. Red is my favorite color." Nick tugged at either side of a large paper ball creation, both of his arms extended wide, and between them, the ball unfolded and expanded into a paper chain of alternating large and small hearts. "I love that woman. I dearly do. So much. She's the one for me; she's a keeper. Married more than thirty years now, can you believe it?" Nick slung the paper heart necklace over his head and across his chest. His hands grabbed at still more crafting supplies with no pause between completed projects. "Josh, is it true what they say about you and your followers—that you never marry? That doesn't seem very heavenly or Godly."

Josh was slowly gluing popsicle sticks together to make a small boat. He clamped the boat between his hands while waiting for it to dry. He closed his eyes to search for the God voice inside his head. "People are in error because they don't know the Scriptures nor the power of God," Josh's voice rose in volume suddenly and echoed in the room. He closed his eyes and felt compelled to repeat the words aloud which he now heard in his head: "In the resurrection to come, we neither will marry nor be given in marriage; we will be like the angels in heaven." Josh placed the boat on the table and began folding pipe cleaners and buttons into two little fishermen to sit in it.

He breathed in, held for 1-2-3, breathed out, then explained it all to Nick, more softly and quietly, in his own words. "Marriage is almost as bad as private property in terms of oppressing humanity. Marriage, monogamy, vow coupling, holy matrimony—whatever you call it—is anything but holy. It is a desecration, an unholy union, an oppression akin to slavery. It encourages possessiveness, exclusivism, indifference, disregard, jealousy, and manipulation." Josh weaved several cut pieces of tan yarn into a single net. "It's marriage that sort of got me in here this time around."

"How so?" Nick grabbed a bundle of pipe cleaners and a mound of buttons and twisted feverishly.

"I have a boyfriend, Yehud. He wants us to marry but he knows how I feel about marriage, how we're all supposed to feel about it. We've become monogamous as it is, which we're not supposed to be in our community. It's an abomination. We're hypocrites!" Josh spread out his tan yarn net on the table near his model boat and put the ends into the hands of his two toy fishermen. "How can I strive to be divine if I love one person over another? That's selfishness."

Nick opened the palm of one hand to reveal a stack of toy fish, button eyes thread through single pipe cleaners, each folded over into two intersecting arcs, with their ends extending beyond the meeting point to resemble the profile of fish. "You know, it's okay to love one person and for them to love you. It may not be divine, as you say, but it's perfectly human. Humans are selfish, love is selfish, humans love." Nick used his other hand to pick up the different colored fish and drop them into Josh's fishing net. "Don't let perfection be the enemy of good. And believe me, real life is good enough. We don't need a Kingdom of Heaven; we just need community here on Earth." Nick took two of his toy fish and interlocked them, showed them to Josh, then dropped them into the net. "And why shouldn't you marry? Even have children if you want. We all fish in the same waters."

Josh grabbed a small box of wooden blocks and began constructing a house on the table near his fishing boat. "Nick, you know what?" He moved his hands across the table and cupped them on top of Nick's jittering fingers, shuttering their motion for a moment. His dark brown eyes met Nick's light blue. "You're a real *mensch*."

Nick smiled and winked. Josh withdrew his hands, and Nick's fingers returned to their rapid fluttering. "This is my last piece. I need to cut out early." Nick's fingers stopped, and his hands lifted to reveal his masterpiece. It was a large toy train engine built from popsicle sticks, pipe cleaners, buttons, rubber bands, cardboard, colored paper, tape, and cork... perhaps an entire cross-section from the art cart in its entirety. He pulled it back to prime the rubber band motor, then released it on the table, where it ran slow circles around Josh's toy house and boat. Josh even heard a small "choo-choo" sound emerge after each rotation. "I need to go check on my socks. They got soaked after my adventure last night, so I hung them out to dry above the radiator in my room." Nick removed a small comb from his pocket and quickly stroked his beard. "Is laundry done here?"

Josh shrugged. "Not exactly. There's a laundry chute behind the nursing station. It falls down to the sub-basement, where there's a big washing machine for the whole hospital. I know because I volunteered to help fold laundry there during my last admission."

Nick stood and leaned over Josh's head to speak privately and quietly—at least quietly for Nick. "Hmmm. Interesting. Okay, I'll see you soon at dinner. Save a space for just us two." He used air quotes for emphasis, "We need to chat about our *plan* for later tonight."

Before Nick walked away, he turned to the short aide at their table and offered his closed hand, dorsal side up. "*Salamat,*" he pronounced slowly. The aide smiled, then bowed and pressed his forehead against Nick's hand.

Nick walked to the door, then stopped himself. "Hey Josh, I almost forgot. What's the best way to gain confidence?" A slight pause as Josh stroked his beard and rolled his eyes. "To *believe in your elf*. Ho, ho, ho. Ha, ha, ha!"

December on 5C4

X

O.T. HOUR HAD NOT QUITE FINISHED yet when Josh felt a fullness in his bowels and bladder. He excused himself and left for the men's bathroom down the hallway. The medication often made him constipated and unable to urinate and he could tell it had worn off because his energy had returned. As did the volume and volubility of the voice in his head.

He sat on the cold seat and mused. *How can we sinful human beings ever hope to justify our lives before a holy God?* The answer came to him in a warming thought, or was it the God voice? Both, he supposed. *We can't. We cannot attain salvation from sin and punishment, but God—God can give it to us and save us.* Josh heard a warm, deep male voice inside himself, echoing into the stall: "My justice is that righteousness by which, through grace and sheer mercy, I justify humanity through faith."

Josh mumbled aloud in awed response, "The Holy Spirit has revealed this truth of the scriptures to me." He finished, wiped, flushed, then returned to his dorm room to wash his hands thoroughly in his room sink. He quickly recited his **asher yatzar bracha**: **"Baruch atah Adonai Elohainu Melech Ha'Olam, asher yatzar et ha'adam b'khochmah, u'vara vo neakvim nekavim, chalulim chalulim. Galuy ve'yadua lifnei khisei khevodekha she'im yipateiach echad meihem, 'o yisateim echad meihem, 'i efshar le'hitkaiyeim ve'la'amod lefaneykha. Baruch atah Adonai, reofi kohl basar u'mafli la'asot."** *Blessed are You, Adonai, our God, King of the universe, who formed man with wisdom and created within him many openings and many hollow spaces. It is obvious and known before Your Seat of Honor that if even one of them were opened, or if even one of them would be sealed, it would be impossible to survive and to stand before You even for one hour. Blessed are You, Adonai, who heals all flesh and acts wondrously.*

Josh walked briskly down the hallway to the common room as the clock turned to 5PM. Five tones trilled through the ward PA system, followed by a man's voice: "Day is done, everyone. Dinner is served now in the canteen."

He stood at the back of a line of other patients as they all waited for the kitchen wall to roll up. It was an impoverished and mostly homeless group of men and women, with two women who were born men and one man who was born a woman. Three were in their twenties, one in her seventies, and most aged somewhat indecipherably in between. Some were parents, and all were children to someone, of course. One rode a wheelchair, two used crutches, and another with dark glasses held a cane. Most were emaciated, three were corpulent. White, brown, yellow, red, and black, their skin tones and races as varied as their misfortunes.

They all had suffered much. Most from *too much*. Too much emotion—sadness, anxiety, anger, even happiness—or too much thought—obsessions, compulsions, delusions, hallucinations. All from too little: too little health, food, money, community, and power. They stood together in their line, but to Josh, they all seemed so separate—lost, lonely, hopeless—as they struggled to survive their illnesses. Many were mumbling incoherently, others shaking and twisting limbs uncontrollably.

Josh remembered some Latin: "*Lacrimae mondi.*" The tears of the world. "*Lacrimae rerum.*" The tears of things.

Did I just speak out loud? Was it me or the voice? Does it even matter anymore?

The metal shutters rolled up from the food service window on the long side of the common room wall. Dinner was lined up as a buffet along the service table ledge beneath the roller window. Josh grabbed a gray tray, plastic cutlery, and a melamine plate. There were cooked carrots, fresh cherry tomatoes, bread rolls, macaroni and cheese, and mint jello at the end. He also poured a large glass of water.

He sat at a small table in the corner that had only two empty chairs and saved the second seat for Nick. He reviewed his meal on the tray and thanked God for it, reciting several **brachot rishonot** for the various foods on his tray. He grabbed his fork and slowly enjoyed the first real meal of his day. He watched as Nick entered late in his red robe and hat. The fat man walked to the meal window where a set of small hands reached up from inside and gave him a bright green tray.

Nick lifted the tray and walked over to sit next to Josh. Several boxes, bags, and large cups all had the golden arches sealed upon them. There were several Big Macs, a large order of french fries, ketchup packets, a tall Coca Cola, and chocolate cookies for dessert.

"So, Josh, after I hung my stockings and combed my beard, I wandered the unit as best I could. As best as I can tell, there is no way out except through those two big red metal front doors. But they don't budge except when the nurses hit the release button at the nursing station, and even then, there's that siren that blares over the PA each time." Nick chewed off half his hamburger in one bite, swallowed, and followed it with a long sip from his cola. "But I was thinking about what you said about that laundry chute. I looked at it from a lot of angles...I'd say it's as big as a chimney, maybe even bigger. If I can climb down a chimney, I can climb down that laundry chute." Nick finished the second half of his first hamburger, then took two french fries, dipped them in ketchup, and slid them into his mouth. "I can climb in with you on top of me. The two of us. And then we get out through the hospital basement."

"Hmmm." Josh nodded his head. "Hmmm." He let another fork of warm macaroni and cheese melt away in his mouth. "Hmmm." He sipped his water and then said, "That sounds like it will work. But there's one problem, Nick. There's a night nurse. The nursing station is manned twenty-four-seven."

Nick opened the wrapper of his next hamburger. "I thought of that—I even asked about it—it's a newer nurse named Mike. They usually have a younger man do the night shifts."

"So?"

"So. We can use Nature to do our work for us. Just show up tonight after lights out. Be upset and say you need to talk for a bit. I'll take care of the rest." Nick ate half a hamburger again in one chew, then swallowed. "Also, when you go there, I need you to ditch your pajamas—just wear your underwear, but keep your sandals on."

"I don't get it."

"You don't have to. You've never had to think about it. I've seen the way some of the male nurses look at you. I've seen the way *everyone* looks at you." Nick reached forward with the palm of his hand and patted Josh on the front of his chest. "You're ripped, Josh. I bet you even have cum gutters."

"What are those?"

"Look, that doesn't matter." Nick grabbed a handful of french fries. "Also, whatever you do, don't take your medicine later; the trick is to palm the pill. Let me show you." Nick swallowed the french fries, emptying both hands. He reached forward with one and picked up a small cherry tomato from Josh's plate. He placed it in the palm of his hand, closed his fingers, opened them, and the cherry tomato had vanished. He closed his fingers again, opened them, and the tomato reappeared.

Nick grabbed both of Josh's hands and held them beneath his own. "The trick I learned from Winter is to fold your thumb over the center so you can hide the coin—or tomato, or pill—beneath your thenar eminence, that's this big fold under your thumb." He placed a small cherry tomato on one of Josh's palms and slowly moved Josh's fingers and thumb to hide it. "Slowed down, Winter's magic does not appear very magical. The magic comes when you speed it up."

Nick sped up the movements, and Josh looked down as the small cherry tomato disappeared into his hand. *Oy Gevalt!* Nick slowed down the movements, and the tomato reappeared. Nick returned it to Josh's plate.

"Keep practicing this after dinner." Nick finished his last hamburger, then slowed down—slow for Nick—to savor his french fries. Josh matched this pace, steadily finishing his meal. He then dipped his fingertips into his cup of water and quickly, in a low mumble, recited the lengthy full **birkat hamazon**, the traditional grace after meals. He made it through the second benediction but was interrupted in the third by an old woman sobbing at the table next to them.

She leaned over and grabbed Josh's sleeve. "My wedding, my wedding out here in Qana. It's ruined. There is no wine here today. They have no wine." The veins popped out from her thin hand as the fingers wrapped around Josh's wrist. There was a small gold ring on her right index finger. She stared at Josh, disoriented, in anguish and distress.

Josh heard the God voice rise inside of him and spoke it aloud, "Let's not be troubled by this, neither you nor me. My hour has not yet come."

Her face softened suddenly, and she stared at Josh with an expression of recognition. "I'll do whatever you say."

"See those six old jars?" Josh felt compelled to point to the row of empty jars on the shelf beneath the snack bench. "Fill them with water."

The woman stood and dumped a bit of her cup of water into each of the jars. An attendant somehow appeared from behind the kitchen window and then poured water from a large pitcher to further fill all six of the jars up to the brim.

The God voice commanded through Josh: "Now let us draw and take drink from these jars."

Josh saw himself stand and walk next to the six jars. He dunked an empty paper cup into the water and lifted it out into the air as a wedding toast. He saw clear water, smelled it, took a sip, and tasted it.

He closed his eyes and centered all his **kavanah**. For Josh and his kin, **kavanah** represented the strength mustered in devotion toward the divine. It is full concentration followed by the truthful perception of a response to faith. *God is here, God listens, God acts*. It is the ecstatic realization that—*I, you, we—all of us* are bonded with God. The actual words of any prayer meant very little compared to the **kavanah** of the one praying it; this mattered most to God.

Josh held out the paper cup of water in one hand, then held the palm of his other hand just over the top. The room fell quiet, and then he spoke his prayer aloud. **"Barukh ata Adonai Eloheinu, Melekh ha'olam, bo're p'ri hagefen."** *Blessed are You, Lord our God, King of the universe, Who creates the fruit of the vine.*

There was silence, then Josh heard a bell, then chimes, then a sudden rushed symphonic stanza of an enormous, ineffable orchestra, then silence.

December on 5C4

With his eyes closed, he moved the cup beneath his nose. He smelled wine. He lifted the cup to his mouth and sipped. He tasted wine. It was delicious, dry, and full-bodied.

Josh opened his eyes and looked down into the cup to see water. But just then, as the sun set outside, a single purple light ray beamed in through the windows above the common room wall and hit the paper cup, briefly causing its contents to flare and glow. Josh blinked from the glare and opened his eyes to see a deep red syrah filling his cup.

He placed the cup on the bench behind him, grabbed the last small dinner roll from the buffet, and held it out before him with two hands on either side. He closed his eyes again, recentered his **kavanah**, then spoke aloud another prayer: "***Barukh ata Adonai Eloheinu, melekh ha'olam, hamotzi lechem min ha'aretz.***" *Blessed are You, Lord our God, King of the universe, Who brings forth bread from the earth.* A last beam of light from the setting sun entered the room via the window and reflected off the bread. Josh heard a few more chimes and bells.

The patients silently stood from their tables and formed a line before Josh. The aides and attendants in the room joined as well. Nick waited, then rose and joined last in the procession.

Josh broke the small roll of bread into two pieces and held them aloft. The God voice compelled him to speak loudly to the crowd: "This is my body, broken for you. Eat this in remembrance of me."

Each person stepped forward slowly and silently as Josh placed half of the small dinner roll into their mouths. He kept breaking the same roll into these halves, but each portion somehow remained the same size as the original whole. Nick was last in line, and for him, his piece of bread transformed into a large, freshly baked chocolate chip cookie.

After eating the bread, the crowd lined up again and quietly stood before Josh. He took a cup and dipped it into one of the jars—to Josh, the water there had somehow become wine, and this wine was also somehow his blood. He held the full cup aloft and listened to words that flowed from his mouth: "This cup is the new covenant in my blood, which is poured out for many. Do this, as often as you drink it, in remembrance of me." Josh drank from the cup. "Truly, I tell you, I will not drink again from the fruit of the vine until that day when I drink it new in the kingdom of God." He grabbed another paper cup and filled it with more blood wine from the jars. He gave a new full cup to each person in the line as they approached. They each then drank it before leaving their place in line. The patients returned to their seats at the tables, and the staff to their various positions.

As before, Nick was last in line. Josh gave him blood wine in his cup, yet Nick somehow drank a half pint of milk. He wiped his lips on the cuff of his red robe.

Josh felt a sudden wave of exhaustion. He leaned onto Nick to steady himself. "Nick, you are God's perfect child. You all are. This table—" Josh waved at the kitchen wall ledge and the snack bench "—this is the table of the Lord, prepared for all. Everyone is invited. All are welcome. May you eat and drink in remembrance of me." Then Josh began crying, tripped a little, and Nick caught him.

Nick held Josh's arm and walked him back to their table. Josh was sweating and breathing heavily and his eyes were glassy. He looked at Nick, who was also looking around.

Josh could hear various dishes clinking and the din of several conversations. Dining hour continued in the community room as if nothing had happened. *Had nothing just happened?* Josh suddenly felt dizzy and nauseous. "I'm sorry Nick. The medicine—it's a twice a day dosing—it's definitely worn off from this morning." Josh arose slowly from the table. "I think I better go lay down for a few minutes in my room before outside time."

Josh shuffled out of the common room toward the long hallway, then stopped himself in the doorway connecting the two. He turned around and gave a soft shout, "Hey Nick, I almost forgot—" Josh giggled to himself, then continued, "What do you call an elf who follows my teachings?"

Nick stroked his beard, then froze with a puzzled expression for several seconds before answering. "Frankly, Josh, I think they'd be *short* of money."

"That's pretty good Nick," Josh replied, then he added some finger air quotes of his own. "But no, quite the opposite: they'd be *welfy* beyond their wildest dreams."

"Ho, ho, ho. Ha, ha, ha." Josh heard Nick's deep belly laugh echo from the common room, down the hallway, and back again. "Ho, ho, ho. Ha, ha, ha."

December on 5C4

JOSH PROPPED HIMSELF UP in his bed and felt better quickly. The nausea and dizziness subsided and his concentration improved. His energy was back. The God voice quieted down, at least for the time being.

He pulled hard on the bottom button of his pajama shirt and plucked it off. He held the small round piece of plastic in his palm. *Just the right size for practice.* He nudged his thumb over slightly to the center of his palm, creating a small ridge, a hidden pocket of sorts, beneath what Nick had called his *thenar eminence*. The small button tucked right in. He rotated and turned his hand as it palmed the button. *From most angles, you can't see the button at all. Nick's friend Winter must be quite the magician.*

Josh sat up in his bed for a good while longer, resting and practicing. If he could reliably palm the small button, then he could reliably palm a small pill. *Later tonight would be the test.*

Josh heard a staccato static. The PA speakers turned on in the unit everywhere, all at once. A short melody on a bassoon played loudly in a very high register before a young man's voice announced, "The courtyard is open now for all patients of 5C4." The bassoon melody repeated, and the man spoke again, "Please come to the nurses' station for outdoor time in the courtyard."

Josh left his dorm and walked down the hallway and through the common room. He stopped in line at the front of the nursing station. Ward 5C4 had a large set of two red metal doors which controlled ingress and egress from the unit. Between these doors and the common room, the nursing station stood as an antechamber. Behind their large gray stone countertop, there were files, phones, the PA system, the door controls, the large laundry chute, and a small door to a private break room with lockers and a half bathroom. The nurses had a few stools on one side, the patients a few chairs on the other.

Josh was last in line in the second group of patients to depart. An aide asked everyone their name, matched it to their name tags, and checked off something on his clipboard. Then he uncoiled a thick hemp rope with five knots tied every few feet. Each patient was asked to grab a knot in their fist and walk forward together, guided by the rope held in the aide's hand. The night nurse behind the countertop pushed the door release button, and a loud alarm bell rang repeatedly. The double red metal doors opened, and the group walked through, then those doors closed behind them, and the alarm bell stopped ringing.

Ward 5C4 opened onto a central atrium inside the hospital. It was enclosed by skylights in the ceiling high above. Josh looked up; they were on the first floor, but there were so many floors above them. It was too much, too soon. Josh was blinded by the lights—too many, too bright, too chaotic—and deafened by the sounds—too many, too loud, too cacophonous. Doctors, nurses, orderlies, patients, and visitors moved quickly in every direction, all at once. Random announcements over the large hospital speakers kept clamoring and interrupting one another. Josh closed his eyes and held onto the rope. He counted. It was a hundred steps left, then fifty steps right, then through another door, and then they were there.

The atrium abutted a similarly sized open-air courtyard in the center of the old hospital. This old courtyard was once the dilapidated domain of cigarette breaks but had long since been remodeled into a central green space. Josh opened his eyes as the door closed behind them. It was indeed a peaceful and relatively pastoral courtyard.

The orderly guarded the door and held the travel rope as the patients were released to wander the garden. Josh began strolling along the figure eight walking path. One loop surrounded a small hill with a large fir tree atop it, the other loop encircled a bubbling freshwater koi pond. The evening air was fresh and cool, and white vapor puffed out briefly after every exhalation.

The hill was powdered by a light sprinkling of snow, and Josh climbed up it toward a dark wooden bench at the base of the large fir. He read the gold plaque affixed to the corner of the bench, *Donated by the Har HaOsher Foundation*. Was that the bench or the whole tree? Josh looked up. And what a whole tree it was. It seemed over two hundred feet tall with a base well over ten feet in diameter. Endless whorls of evergreen branches spiraled upward around the center trunk. The bark was dark brown with thick ridges. The tree had needles instead of leaves which were a waxy dark greenish blue, encircling and coating every twig over nearly every branch. There were brown pine cones of all sizes scattered in the branches and on the grounds below. A minty smell wafted everywhere nearby.

This tree inspired the same awe in Josh now as it did with every visit. He centered his **kavanah** and offered thanks for this miracle. "**Barukh ata Adonai Eloheinu, melekh ha'olam, she'lo chisar b'olamo klum u'vara vo beri'ot tovot ve'ilanot tovim le'hanot bahem benei adam.**" *Blessed are You, Lord our God, King of the universe, Who left out nothing in His world and created pleasant creations and* *good trees so that people can derive benefit from them.*

      A wind suddenly gusted inside the courtyard. It swirled around and around the enormous fir tree, rising upward and dislodging a blanket of white snow from the top branches. The snowpack fell to reveal the fir tree in its full verdant majesty. The tree seemed somehow taller, stronger, and even prouder than ever.

      Josh looked up to the top of the tree and watched as it faded into the darkening sky as twilight turned to dusk. A scattering of small stars began twinkling across the dark blue sky. Suddenly, Josh witnessed an unusually large and bright star in the eastern sky above the tree top. It was but for a moment, but it blinked brightly, then dimmed itself. Josh yelled in startled amazement, "*Oy gevalt!*" Then he prayed quietly in gratitude, "**Barukh ata Adonai Eloheinu, melekh ha'olam, o'seh ma'ase be'reshit.**" *Blessed are You, Lord our God, King of the universe, Who re-enacts the work of creation.*

      The courtyard was now much darker, and garden lights popped on all around the pathway. Several large spotlights illuminated the tree from beneath. Josh turned and looked down upon the pond from the top of the hill. A rainbow of red, green, and blue underwater lights made the bubbling waters glow. Josh walked down the hill and returned to the walking path, then ambled over to the loop encircling the pond. It was an enormous oval of bubbling freshwater with a shore of large stones, small bushes, and layers of white pebbles. Josh stood over the pond and looked down upon the silver and gold speckled backs of a family of ancient koi squiggling and squirming in the depths below. The water spewed an earthy and musty aroma. The water pumps buried beneath the pond rumbled with a low hum, and the bubbles and waves atop the water swished and splashed. A small spotlight in the ground illuminated a plaque affixed to a large stone in front of the pond— *Donated by the Tiberias Family*. Josh paused to give thanks to his fellow man, "Thank you, Tiberias Family," and as always, to God. "**Baruch ata Adonai Eloheinu, melekh ha'olam, she'asa et ha'yam ha'gadol.**" *Blessed are You, Lord our God, King of the universe, Who made the large bodies of water.*

      With the end of his prayer, the fish stopped their many random movements and somehow lined up single file in an orderly circle beneath the waters. *Maybe they're waiting for food?* A gold topped koi rose and briefly broke the surface with its head. The lidless eyes met Josh's gaze. An eye with no lids, an eye always wide open, never blinking, and thus all-seeing. To Josh and his people, the fish was a symbol for God's omniscience. Each year on the afternoon of **Rosh Hashanah**, the Jewish New Year, after the **Mincha** service, Josh as a child would walk with his family to the nearby park along the Yarden River. There, they would complete a ritual called ***tashlikh***, meaning *casting off*. During this, they would symbolically cast off their sins from the previous year by tossing breadcrumbs or pebbles into the water. Josh had no breadcrumbs, but he bent low and scooped up a handful of white pebbles from the shore. He plucked a pebble from the pile, held it between his fingers, closed his eyes, concentrated on his recent sins, then dropped the stone into the pond. As he watched the pebble—and his sin—sink into the watery depths, he mumbled a quote from Micah, "You will cast all their sins into the depths of the sea." He dropped another and another. *A hundred pebbles for a hundred sins, and each cleansed by these watery depths. Sins forgiven, but are they ever forgotten, and should they be?*

God sees all sins. God sees all. This omniscience had always been a problem for Josh. God is omniscient, omnipotent, and omnibenevolent. He is all-seeing, all-powerful, and all-good. The problem was that two out of any three were possible on Earth, but the concurrency of all three was a logical inconsistency. Josh's faith, however—both the old and the new—demanded all three. This, indeed, was a divine mystery.

He was down to one remaining pebble, but rather than drop it into the pond, he palmed it in his hand. *Just like that, I can make the pebble vanish.* Josh had mastered Nick's trick of folding over his thumb and tucking the pebble into the ridge. *Just like that, imagine if I could make sin vanish as well.*

"Ho, ho, ho. Ha, ha, ha." His musings were interrupted by Nick's distinctive laugh from across the courtyard.

Josh turned around at the base of the pond and looked up the hill toward the fir tree atop it. Nick was on the wooden bench near the tree trunk. The large, fat man was sitting there in his red robe and hat, crafting something with both hands.

Josh approached him along the walking path from below. "Nick, look at my empty hands." Josh held the palms of his hands forward for inspection. He then closed his hand into a fist, waved the other over it, and reopened the fist. "*Da iz es!*" A small pebble was in the palm of his hand.

"Oh, that's fine work. Winter would be proud." Nick chuckled and smiled.

Josh closed his fingers over the pebble and made a fist again, waved his hand over it, then reopened the fist, "*Vu iz es!*" The pebble had vanished. "Do you think I'm ready for tonight?"

Nick nodded and smiled, then returned to crafting on the bench. He was weaving together several pliable branches from the fir tree. He circled them around and braided them into one another to form a decorative ring of dark greenish-blue needles, twigs, red berries, and even a few pinecones.

"Josh, if you are who I think you are, then you are a king amongst your people. And so I've made you this crown." Nick stood in front of Josh and held the finished garland aloft with both hands, holding it over and above Josh's head. "It's your birthday tomorrow. Can I give this to you as a present, now? I mean, if I agree to give *everyone* else a present, too, then it'd be fair, right?"

Josh felt the God voice rise inside him with a reply, "Truly I tell you, whatever you give to the least of my brothers and sisters, you give to me." He nodded, then turned around and allowed Nick to crown him. "Give, and it will be given to you." And then somehow, that star from before, the one in the eastern sky above the tree top, shined brightly, expanded, and then dimmed once again. Both Nick and Josh were startled by this momentary flare.

Nick bellowed from behind Josh, "To celebrate Josh's birthday tomorrow, I will give everyone who has been good this year a present, even a Myra toy if you want one! Just come sit by me and whisper what you'd like into my ear." Nick rotated his wrist and checked the time on his gold wristwatch. "I even promise to get them to each of you by tomorrow morning!"

NICK SAT AGAIN ON THE WOODEN BENCH next to the magnificent fir tree. Josh stood nearby, behind the bench and beneath the tree. He wore the crown—a wreath of thorns—upon his head. It looked barbed and itchy, but it was actually quite smooth and soft as Nick's craftsmanship was exceptional.

The various other patients from 5C4, who all had been wandering the courtyard, began to migrate along the walking path toward Nick on his bench.

"So, Josh, may we sing you Happy Birthday tomorrow?"

"My people don't normally do that."

"What do you all do then?"

"We say '*Bis hundert aun tzvantzig*' to each other. It means *until one-hundred-twenty*. It's shortened from '*may you live until one hundred and twenty years old.*' The prophet Moses died at the age of one hundred twenty, so we view long life and good health as a reward for righteous behavior." Josh placed both hands on the bench's backrest as he stood behind Nick. He leaned down a bit and confessed, "That's why I am so frustrated that God wants me to die at thirty-three. Either I'm not going to get the reward, or worse, I'm not very righteous."

"I don't know about any of that, Josh." Nick turned in his seat and placed both his hands over Josh's, then gave a quick squeeze. "But, *bis hundert aun tzvantzig!*"

Just then, two squirrels darted out from the fir, chittering on the ground, chasing each other in fanciful spirals up and around the tree trunk. Several pinecones dislodged and tumbled down with a few twigs from above. Nick instinctively raised his hand and caught one from above, all while still looking forward, down at the pond. He briefly admired the pinecone and then gave it to Josh.

"What about gifts, Josh? Did you get presents on your birthdays?"

"Not exactly, kind of the opposite, actually." Josh rolled the pinecone in his hands. "Many of us believe that on our birthdays, they have mystical powers—it's called *ascending fortune*. Time is a spiral. On the anniversary of any momentous event, we can tap into the same spiritual energy that originally caused that specific event. And, of course, everyone's birth is a momentous event—it's the day God decided the universe could no longer exist without them! So it's actually our custom to ask for blessings from anyone who is about to celebrate their birthday."

"Well then, can you give us all blessings?" The squirrels continued their battle, knocking another pinecone from the tree. Nick lifted his hand and, again, caught the falling pinecone with minimal effort.

"Of course. It's always more blessed to give than to receive." Josh returned the first pinecone to Nick and stood straight behind him on his bench, the homemade wreath still secure on his head.

An obese young woman with mismatched shoes—one a boot, the other a sneaker—walked up the hill toward the men. She sat down next to Nick on the wooden bench and leaned in and whispered into his ear.

Josh noticed the fresh bandages wrapped around her wrists. Then, there was an electric jolt from the wreath on his head. He twitched a bit, then froze. This was something new, different from the God voice—it was more like a God... *vision*. In a flash, Josh saw and knew. He saw everything about this woman, and he knew everything about her. It was like a seizure of omniscience:

...the rapes by my uncle when I was a girl... ...coming out to my parents... ...getting kicked out of the house.... .... a teen runaway in the city... ...the break-up with my girlfriend... ...months of such overwhelming sadness... ...loneliness... ... hopelessness... ...calling her... ...writing that note...

Josh held out his hands above the woman, forming the fingers of each hand into a V: two sets of two fingers to each side, with spaces between his ring fingers and his middle fingers. He pushed his two thumbs towards each other, touching at the knuckles. His hands each now formed a Hebrew letter **shin**, an emblem for ***El Shaddai***, a name of God best translated as *God Almighty*. Josh summoned his ***kavanah*** as his hands seemed to luminesce with a soft white glow. He recited aloud the blessing, which the God voice shared with him: "Blessed are the poor in spirit, for theirs is the Kingdom of Heaven."

An old man arrived to change places with the woman. He, too, whispered into Nick's ear. Josh saw the man's enormous glasses and the puffy red eyes behind them. Another electric jolt from the wreath on his head. And again, Josh suddenly saw and knew. Everything, everything about this man.

...a marriage of forty-one years... ...the pension fund is insolvent... ...choosing between food or medicine... ...the dementia which takes hold of my wife... ...locked memory care units are too expensive... I fall asleep, and she wanders off... she is found frozen dead weeks later... ...the guilt is too much... ...I cannot sleep anymore... ...the world is not safe... ...don't leave the apartment... ...I draw my kitchen knife at the social workers who come to

check on me...

Josh kept his glowing hands connected by the thumbs, holding them out as two Hebrew letter **shins** above the seat next to Nick. He summoned more **kavanah** and recited again loudly more of what the God voice shared, "Blessed are those who mourn, for they will be comforted."

Next, a young man sat next to Nick, he too whispered in Nick's ear, but he could not turn his head to meet Nick's gaze. He kept his hands near his head and in front of his eyes to block anyone from looking directly at his face. Josh felt another eclectic jolt and another zap of omniscience. The God vision showed him all there was to know about this young man.

...shyness... ...new people are terrifying... ...only mommy is safe... ...I get anxious... ...avoid things that make me uncomfortable, then some things, then everything, then everybody... ...alcohol makes me brave... ... I need to work to buy alcohol because I need to buy alcohol to work... ...always more alcohol... ...the accident at the loading site... I drink alcohol with the new pills so I can be brave for court... ...I wake up in the ambulance...

Josh held his glowing hands frozen in position. He gathered still more **kavanah** and gave another pronouncement from the God voice within him: "Blessed are the meek, for they will inherit the Earth."

The young man was followed by a glamorous middle-aged woman. She wore a brown faux fur stole over a black evening gown, with kitten heel shoes. She had luxurious blond hair tied in a braid, with tinted eyebrows to accent her bright blue eyes. Her dress showed her shoulders and cleavage, and Josh noted how she had an unnaturally even full-body tan. She placed her arm over Nick's shoulders and leaned forward to whisper. Josh noted how large her wrists were and heard how deep her whisper rumbled. Then he looked at her neck and noted how prominent her larynx bulged forward. She was a he, at least biologically. Josh was again zapped by the God vision, and, in that flash, he knew her life as if it were his own.

...I am a girl born with a penis... ...if I stay thin enough, I can be a girl, be loved, and have control... ...I can eat all I want and then just vomit it out... ...I am passing... ...my teeth are falling out... ...they will fire me if they find out... ...I almost have enough saved for surgery... ...I need to eat to live, but to live I can't eat... ...I faint on the subway...

His hands glowed and cast the light of two large **shins** down above the woman's head. He felt so much **kavanah** that it was overpowering, as he loudly proclaimed more from his God voice: "Blessed are those who hunger and thirst for righteousness, for they will be satisfied."

The woman gave Nick a small kiss on his cheek, then rose to give her seat to a muscular man with crutches and a prosthetic leg. He sat down and placed his crutches beneath Nick's bench. He bent over to whisper into Nick's ear but also to outline something for Nick on the palm of his hand with a finger. His face had fresh scars from multiple small cuts. The God vision bolted through Josh's body with a stutter. His head, arms, and legs shuttered, but he managed to keep his hands aloft in the blessing position. Josh instantly lived everything about this man.

…there is no hope for my future out here in the country… …no money to be made… …being a soldier means food, shelter, clothing, money, and education… …the war… …the little girl was screaming for help, so I brought her to our base… …a bomb vest and then all of my brothers dead… …why did I survive… …every sound makes me jump… …I am dangerous to others… …the waitress, her daughter, she looks like, is she the little girl?… …I move to strike her, I push my own head through the window to stop myself… …where am I?... …when am I?... …make it all stop!...

Josh gazed down at his glowing hands and the large shadow they projected over the man's head. He channeled his **kavanah** into yet another blessing from God, "Blessed are the merciful, for they will be shown mercy."

The man lifted his crutches, rose and rebalanced, then moved out along the path. Next to sit was a chubby brown man with curly gray hair and small glasses. He wore a fully buttoned blue dress shirt with matching navy pants. He walked toward the bench, then walked backward three steps, 1-2-3, then forward three steps, 1-2-3, then mumbled aloud, "1-2-3," then turned and sat down, clenching both hands together at his waist. He whispered to Nick but stared straight ahead throughout. Josh felt more sparks ignite inside him. The God vision then showed Josh the man's life as if it were his own.

…no school for two weeks because I have a sore throat… …I don't want to harm anyone… …If I think a bad thought, then something bad will happen… ….my baby cousin dies… …I need to think good thoughts when I see a baby or they will get cancer and die... …Puppies and kittens, too… …pray three times to be sure... ...tap three times… …three will protect me... …Did I do it three times?… …three more times to be sure… …Then three more… …I doubt… …how can I be certain… …I am trapped in my doorway… …I can't move or someone will die… …I pee in my pants……Auntie comes days later and rescues me…

Josh's hands vanished, replaced by two blazing **shins**. **Shin** for **Shaddai, El Shaddai**, God Almighty. He focused the **shins** over the chubby man's curly hair as he focused more **kavanah**, and this amplified yet another blessing from the God voice within, "Blessed are the pure in heart, for they will see God."

The chubby man stood and walked again along the path, forwards three steps, 1-2-3, then backward three steps, 1-2-3, then mumbled aloud, "1-2-3," then walked more regularly into the distance. He was replaced by a buxom, freckled, redheaded woman who slipped right into his seat after he rose. She curled up next to Nick, placing both arms over his head and shoulders and draping both her legs over and onto his lap. She wore a white tee-shirt, gray sweatpants, and black sandals. The tee-shirt was taut against her large breasts, and there was no bra beneath. It was cut to reveal her midsection. Josh noted that the piercing on her belly button matched the piercings in her tongue, under her nose, and the many on each ear. The top sides of her forearms were coated with freckles, but Josh noted how each underside was creamy white but with a line of small scarred-up blue-brown puncture wounds between each wrist and the pit of each elbow. The woman licked her lips, then whispered into Nick's ear. Josh felt the painful discharge of the God vision convulsing through him. In a flash, he lived the woman's life as his own.

...I smile but mommy doesn't smile back... ...the universe is chaos and I can't trust it... ...people are all good or all bad... ...I need to feel something and prove this is all real... ...I can't stop cutting and burning my legs... ...Rudy keeps me safe... ...he gives me drugs when I have sex with his friends, then with other people... ...these drugs give me peace... ...I give peace to these men... ...there can be no peace if mommy doesn't smile back... ...too many men and too many drugs...

Josh breathed in and smelled what he supposed was expensive perfume. The glow from his hands flickered a bit, and he refocused his **kavanah**. He circled his hands above the woman's head, his **kavanah** lifted again the God voice from within him, then he recited yet another pronouncement: "Blessed are the peacemakers, for they will be called children of God."

The woman gave Nick a kiss on his lips, then squeezed and tugged playfully at his hands and arms as she walked away. The last patient in the courtyard came next. She approached more slowly than the others, shuffling quickly but then stopping every few steps to look from side to side. She sat on the bench next to Nick, but not near him, allowing a foot of distance between their bodies. She wore no make-up and had long black hair and blue eyes with dark circles beneath them—a rather noticeable sagging and swelling in her lower eyelids. She cupped both hands around her mouth and then leaned over measuredly to whisper softly into Nick's ear. An electric charge zapped from Josh's head to his toes, then up again and out through his eyes as the God vision's omniscience had him suddenly live this woman's life.

...my husband lost his job and has to work so far away now... ...he sends money but is away when the new baby is born... ...I am so sad... ...the baby doesn't sleep... ...I can't sleep... ...the baby doesn't stop crying... ...I can't stop crying... ...I am so alone... ...how do I protect the baby... ...the television and radio are sending me secret messages... ...they are out to get us... ...they are out to get me... ...we are hunted... ...I need to save the baby... ...I need to give it back... ...I came to the hospital to return the baby but now they won't let me return...

Josh looked down at his glowing hands held above this woman's head.

December on 5C4

His fingers were stiff, but per his people's custom he kept them rigidly in the shape of **shin**, thumbs connected at the knuckles. The two **shins** spread the light of God Almighty, **El Shaddai, shin** for **Shaddai**, for all to bear witness. Josh's **kavanah** shone so brightly through his hands, like the light of the world. He was pleased to let it shine before others so that they might see his good deeds and glorify God. "Blessed are those who are persecuted because of righteousness, for theirs is the Kingdom of Heaven."

No further 5C4 patients came to whisper in Nick's ear, so Josh stood up on his toes to hover his hands over Nick's red cap. Though he knew they were in a garden, Josh suddenly smelled the distinct odor of burning metal, rubber, and plastic all mixed together. It was an electric-like fire inside his mind, and his eyes were inflamed suddenly and briefly by this fire of God's vision. For a moment, he and Nick were one.

…I am so fat… …they hate me because I am fat… …I am so sad, but when I make jokes, they like me… …the girls are repulsed by me… …Jessica loves me even though I am so fat… …losing Jessica, and the baby, in childbirth… …I miss her so much… …darkness… …I see elves, everywhere, and they love me and listen to me… …others say she is gone but the elves believe me… …the silver ring is still on my hand… …if I stay at work, if I travel for work, then I never go home and then she can still be there……the cocaine lets me work even harder… …I am the boss now… …I am rich now… …they love me because I am rich… …Jessica loved me for me…

Lacrimae mondi, the tears of the world, it was an overwhelming sadness. Josh wept. He stumbled forward on his tiptoes behind the bench where Nick was sitting and folded his glowing hands softly over Nick's red cap and head. The God voice surged within him, and Josh loudly proclaimed, "Blessed are you when people insult you, persecute you, and falsely say all kinds of evil against you because of me." The God voice then had him add more, "Rejoice and be glad, because great is your reward in heaven, for in the same way they persecuted the prophets who were before you."

The God vision blurred, and the God voice muffled, and soon there was just Josh standing there wearing his wreath, in his white pajamas and sandals, standing behind Nick, with his hands resting on Nick's cap. Nick kept his gaze forward, out into the courtyard, and looking down upon the pond lights below. Josh's hands were still in the shape of **shins**, glowing softly, though dimming, his **kavanah** still stirred. He closed his eyes and focused this **kavanah** on Nick, then added the other fellow patients, then everyone on 5C4, then in the hospital, then expanded to his followers in the city, everybody in the land, everyone in our world, all humanity, us.

Josh loved the **Birkat Kohanim**, the priestly blessing, this **Nesi'at**

Kapayim, this lifting of hands, and he resolved to give this divine hug to all the world. He sang it slowly and steadily, loudly and mellifluously. "***Yivarechecha Adonai viyishmirecha***" *May the Lord bless you, and keep you.* "***Ya'er Adonai panav elecha veechuneka***" *May the Lord make his face to shine upon you, and be gracious unto you.* "***Yeesa Adonai panav elecha viyasem lecha shalom***" *May the Lord lift up His countenance, and grant you peace.*

A strong wind gusted in the dusk, and Josh heard a chorus of voices susurrate in and amongst the branches and needles of the fir tree above. **Sim Shalom**, Grant Peace, **Sim Shalom**, they sang. His eyes were puffy from his tears. His real vision darkened suddenly from the sides, then the center. His real hearing heard a whooshing sound. Everything went black, and he fell.

When Josh awoke, he found himself seated next to Nick on the large wooden bench beneath the fir tree. He was leaning onto the fat man's side with his head resting gently upon his shoulder. Josh slowly opened his eyes and stared at the man's hands. Nick somehow had a clipboard with paper and a pen and was scribbling rapidly.

"Uhmmm," Josh mumbled himself awake and lifted his head. "Nick, what are you doing?"

"I am making a list and checking it twice."

"But where'd you get the clipboard from? The paper, the pen, your stuff in general?"

"Ho, ho, ho. Ha, ha, ha." Nick laughed loudly, and Josh watched closely as his big belly bounced in and out with each eruption of chuckling. "You fainted, you know. Before you woke up just now, one of my elves gave it to me. He was climbing up this big fir tree right here above us." Nick pointed upward with the index finger of a gloved hand; his hands somehow had white gloves now. "I saw him, only me, and we chatted a bit."

"Really, what'd you say?"

Nick turned his left palm upward. "I said, 'Hey elf, thanks for the stuff, but why are you climbing up this here tree?'" Then Nick turned his right palm upward. "He said, 'Because I want to eat some pears.'" Nick leaned to the left, "So I said, 'What? Don't you know, that's a fir tree—it doesn't grow pears!'" Then he leaned to the right, "He tugged at the little red sack over his shoulder, and then said to me, 'That's okay boss, I brought my own!'"

"Ho, ho, ho. Ha, ha, ha." Nick chuckled. Josh smiled and joined in the laughter.

They sat together silently for a good while after. Nick finished making and checking his list as dusk became darkness. Eventually, the pond lights and pathway lighting all blinked on and off, slowly, over and over. The aide at the courtyard

December on 5C4

doorway shouted and waved that it was time for everyone to come back inside.

Nick and Josh stood up, and Nick placed his arm over Josh's shoulders as they walked down the garden path toward the courtyard doorway. "Josh, before we head in, remember the plan. Palm your medicine tonight like I showed you—don't take it—then come to the nurse's station at lights out, 9PM, and tell them you can't sleep and want to talk a bit." Nick reached under the sleeve of his red robe with one hand and revealed a delicious ripe green pear. He took a bite. "And oh yeah, be sure to ditch your shirt first." He offered the pear to Josh, who took a bite too, then grabbed the whole pear for himself.

Josh finished it. He was so hungry that he even forgot to thank God for this fruit with the traditional *ha'etz* blessing.

For the next few hours, the ward allowed free time for all, phone calls for some, and family visits for others. 5C4 staff encouraged reading and journaling and later enforced evening medications. Josh relaxed for a time, then remembered to palm the red pill they offered him. He tucked it deep into the fleshy pocket he had learned to create inside his hand by bending his thumb inward slightly. He also raised the pill cup with the same hand, pretending to swallow the pill from the empty cup, followed by the distractor of sipping water from a larger cup in his other hand.

Not taking the pill turned out to be no problem at all.

The problem turned out to be underwear. Specifically, Josh not wearing any, and Nick needing him to.

Most consider underwear a necessity, but for Josh and his followers, they considered it an unnecessary luxury. Whenever outreach workers or kind-hearted citizens came through the underpass with care packages of underwear and socks, Josh and his followers either swapped these garments for food to give to the poor, exchanged them for money to give to the poor, or simply gave the clothing directly to the poor. *It's been over a decade since I've worn any underwear at all.*

Josh nevertheless followed Nick's instructions. He closed the door to his dorm room right before lights out. He stood at the foot of his cot and looked at himself in the oval mirror above his sink. He slowly removed his shirt. He slowly removed his pants. A man stood naked before him. This man was he.

Josh had rarely seen his own nakedness. Leviticus prohibited revealing nakedness, including one's own. And so, out of respect for God, who is everywhere and thus sees all, your body must be covered. The general rule in his old community was that you could be nude only when necessary. For the first half of his life, Josh would undress under his bed covers, shower naked, and then dress again under his bed covers. He had been naked in the shower and at the **mikvah**, the ritual bath, but that was it.

However, in Genesis, "Adam and his wife were both naked, and they felt no shame." Josh and his followers preferred Genesis to Leviticus and celebrated their nakedness. *We are God's perfect creations, He loves us just the way we are, and so He adores every part of us that makes us human.* Over the years, Josh and his followers had often been naked around each other, especially in their tent compound, but they never had even a single mirror amongst them, so Josh could not remember the last time he had seen his own nakedness.

But Josh saw his nakedness now, there, in the oval mirror. His body had transformed over the years, shedding the fat of adolescence for the muscle of adulthood. His chest was coated in dark brown curly hair with firm pectoral muscles stretched beneath. The right side of his chest had a long scar along the lower border from an old stabbing. The curly hair from his chest receded to the sides of his abdomen, which was flat, with three rows and two columns of deeply cut and well-grooved muscles. The curly hair then advanced again to surround his pelvis, hiding his testicles beneath the drape of his penis, which was circumcised at the tip as per the custom of his birth. His arms and legs also were coated with dark curly hair, but less densely than his chest and pelvis. Each one of these limbs bulged with clear, prominently toned, and defined muscles. He took a few moments to alternatively tense the muscles of his arms and legs and noted how each swelled like small balloons.

He inspected the hands and feet of each limb. The palm of each of his hands had a single faint round scar in its center from an old puncture wound, as did the dorsum of each foot. He held his head forward to keep his gaze in the mirror but turned his body around as best he could to inspect his backside. His back was broad with several layers of muscles—it was less hairy than his chest, though still much hairier than his belly. Overall, his skin had remained smooth, with an even olive-brown tone everywhere.

He looked again at his pelvis. For traditional Jews, shame and honor were opposites. And so, any clothing which covers nudity brings honor by removing that shame. Josh was once a traditional Jew, though clearly now he had become something else. *Once a Jew, always Jewish.* He had no underwear, but he did have understanding. Josh closed his eyes, remembered a prayer from his **Birchot hashachar**, and invoked the words, "**Baruch atah Adonoi Eloheinu, melech ha'olam, malbish 'arumim.**" *Blessed are You, Lord our God, King of the universe, Who clothes the naked.*

He opened his eyes, and they immediately were guided down to his bedside where a long, thin, white hospital-issued bath towel extended over a railing. He grabbed the flat and frayed towel with both hands across the width and ripped it horizontally across the center, down to the opposite edge, then folded and rolled it to the length of thin towel. He rolled this towel-rope through his crotch and around his legs and buttocks and over to cover his pelvis, tying it into a knot, all to make an efficient loincloth.

Josh slid his feet into his frayed brown leather sandals. They had thin, worn soles with thick center thongs, which pushed each big toe inwards and the smaller toes outwards. He wrapped and then tied a leather strap from each thong up and around both ankles. Next, he donned the gift of Nick's wreath back upon his head. Finally, fully attired for his imminent adventure with Nick, he marched to the small sink in his room and stared deeply into the mirror above it.

I'll be thirty-three years old when I wake up tomorrow morning. Not young anymore, but not old either.

Josh saw long brown hair tied back in a knot, a still wrinkleless round face with soft oval brown eyes, a large nose with thick nostrils, and wide thin lips, all outlined by a chest-length long brown beard. Josh saw himself, but he also saw his father. *I have my father's eyes and my father's beard.* He kissed two fingers on his right hand, then touched them to the eyes and beard reflected in the mirror.

And maybe I have my father's crown, too? Josh lowered his head and circled all around, peering upwards to admire the arbor crown, the wreath Nick had gifted him. It was remarkable craftsmanship. Nick had braided together thirteen long branches from the fir tree to form a thick circlet of dark greenish-blue needles, all decorated with red berries and a few pinecones. Josh held his head straight towards the mirror and focused on the wreath atop his head—he remembered his father's fur crown, his *shtreimel*, worn upon his father's head.

The married men of Josh's community all wore large dark fur hats called *shtreimel*. To wear a *shtreimel* was to wear a crown. It was their most costly article of clothing and customarily a gift from father-in-law to son-in-law as a wedding present. The *shtreimel* is a large circular hat, usually made from thirteen fur tails wrapped clockwise spirally to symbolize the Thirteen Attributes of Mercy from Exodus—the divine attributes by which God governs the world. The hat is lined with black velvet and leather and worn on **Shabbos** and other holy days.

Legend has it that long ago, an evil king decreed that male Jews must wear an animal tail on their heads on **Shabbos**. It was an obvious attempt to mock the Jews, but Jewish law requires they uphold the laws of any land in which they live, as long as those laws do not obstruct ritual observance. The Jews complied, making elaborate royal hats to wear from rings of animal tails, which they then wore proudly. A mark of persecution was changed into a symbol of pride.

Josh lifted his hands to trace the outline of the wreath upon his head. It was his crown tonight, the same size and shape as any *shtriemel*, and just as soft despite being made from branches and needles. *This wreath is my shtriemel, turning persecution into pride.*

The PA speaker squealed, then a young man's voice spoke: "It's 9PM everyone, time for lights out." Several stanzas of a classic lullaby began broadcasting as the man sang matching lyrics along to the melody: "Good evening, good night, with roses covered, with cloves adorned, slip under the covers. Tomorrow morning, you will wake once again."

Josh turned off the light, left his room, and shuffled down the hall to the nursing station. He meandered through the common room, then sat on an old metal chair next to the stone countertop of the nursing station.

"I can't sleep," Josh stated slowly and softly. The metal chair wobbled a bit from one damaged leg. Josh slumped his head down to his chest, placed both hands in his lap, and stared emptily into his palms, rocking himself and the chair back and forth.

"Let's talk it out, okay." The night nurse was behind the counter. "Just give me a moment." He finished writing something in a chart, then closed the notebook and placed it on the rack behind him. He unlocked the half-door to the back of the countertop, left it open, and exited from behind. He grabbed a matching metal seat from across the hall and slid it within a foot of Josh. He reversed the seat and sat at a side angle to Josh.

"My name is Mike," he leaned back a bit and pointed to the name tag attached to his shirt. It was a laminate hospital ID tag with his photo above his first and last name, however, per the custom of nurses on the psychiatric units, his last name was hidden by black electrical tape. "I'm the new night nurse here. I'm kind of new in general."

Mike sat astride the backward chair, with his arms above the top of the back seat and his head resting above it. He was a stocky, fair-skinned young man. His brown, spiky hair had blond highlights, and his right ear was pierced with a small silver stud. He wore a faint mauve underliner above and below his blue eyes. He had a lavender V-neck scrub shirt with dark purple bottom pants. Around his neck, he wore a silver necklace with a two-inch diameter chrome ring hanging through it and dangling as a pendant. A large dark blue handkerchief puffed out of the right chest pocket of his scrub shirt.

"There is so much—" Josh began but stopped himself.

"So much what, Josh?"

"So much pain and suffering in the world. And so much of it is caused by people misunderstanding one another and not forgiving one another."

Mike placed one hand on Josh's naked shoulder and patted it a bit, "That's heavy to think about when you're trying to fall asleep. I'm surprised your medicine hasn't knocked you out already. Want me to get you some more?"

Josh was not sure how to answer. This nurse was so kind and caring. Josh stared deep into his blue eyes, though he did notice, as Nick had predicted, that the man's gaze kept veering involuntarily down to Josh's chest and abdomen. As he always did, Josh told the truth. "No, that's okay, I think I should just talk a bit, but I'm not sure how."

The nurse kept one hand on Josh's shoulder and slid the other into one of Josh's open palms. Josh returned to staring into his hands. They sat like this for a long while. Josh was nearly naked except for his loincloth, the sandals on his feet, and the wreath of needles on his head. Josh continued frowning silently, and Mike alternatively patted him on the back or rubbed his shoulder.

Finally, it was Mike who broke the silence. "Sometimes it helps to be more specific." The night nurse returned his hands to the top of the chair and rested his chin upon them. Mike leaned over a bit to Josh, "Who do you think about for yourself when you think about someone you misunderstand or who misunderstands you?"

Yehud. Josh whispered, then spoke his name, "Yehud, I—"

"Ho, ho, ho. Ha, ha, ha!" Nick's laughter came from the common room and was quickly followed by the man himself wearing his red robe and matching hat. He somehow had a silver serving tray between his hands, and upon it were two mugs of hot chocolate, a glass of milk, and a plate with several chocolate chip cookies and some small carrots. He walked to Josh and Mike and gently placed the tray on the counter.

Nick pointed to the glass and the plate. "Sorry, I was just finishing up a bedtime snack." The glass of milk was mostly drunk, the cookies mostly eaten, and the carrots half-chewed. "But I heard you two over here, so I brought you each a present—some hot cocoa just the way my wife Jessica used to make it."

Nick handed a mug to Josh. "Yours is this one with the marshmallows on top. I remember how much you like them from our chat at dinner." Nick winked at Josh, then addressed the night nurse, "Here's yours, Mike. Don't worry if the chocolate looks a bit reddish, I crushed a peppermint candy stick to add some spice—it makes it delicious."

"Thanks Nick," Josh grabbed his cup of hot chocolate with both hands and placed it beneath his nose, inhaling the aroma with his large nostrils. It was a warm sweetness but also deep, dark, and rugged. He closed his eyes and mumbled a quick **bracha rishona**, before enjoying the chocolaty drink: "**Baruch atah Adonai Eloheinu Melech ha'olam, shehakol nih'yeh bidvaro.**" *Blessed are You, Adonai, our God, King of the Universe, by whose word everything comes to be.* Then Josh sipped and savored the thick beverage.

The night nurse grabbed his cup with one hand, confirmed the temperature with the pinky of the other, and then took a large gulp. "Delicious. I can't quite place the peppermint flavor, but there is something in it that's very

December on 5C4

distinctive. This is yummy. I mean, it's really good. Thanks, Nick."

"Hey, I have a knock-knock joke for you two." Nick stayed standing by the nursing station countertop as Josh and Mike sat in their chairs and finished their drinks. "Knock-knock."

The two were silent.

"Come on, you have to ask, 'who's there?'"

Mike finished the rest of his drink and yawned. "Okay, who's there?" He yawned more.

"Egg"

Mike's shoulders slumped, his head tilted, and his eyes closed. He managed to mumble the traditional reply, "Egg who?"

"*Eggstremely* tired and sleepy." Nick walked over next to Mike's chair just in time as the night nurse passed out. He fell over in his seat, but Nick caught him and quietly lowered him onto the floor.

Josh stood up and placed his half-empty cup of cocoa on the nursing station countertop. He rushed out a quick ***bracha acharona***, after blessing, for the hot chocolate. "***Baruch atah Adonai Eloheinu Melech ha'olam borei nefashot rabot v'chesronan al klol ma she'barata l'hachayot bahem nefesh kol chai. Baruch chei ha'olamim.***" *Blessed are You, Adonai our God, King of the universe, Creator of numerous living beings and their needs, for all the things You have created with which to sustain the soul of every living being. Blessed is He who is the Life of the world.*

Nick looked upwards toward Josh. He was now wearing his white gloves from before. He extended an index finger in front of his pursed lips and gave a soft "Shhh." Then, for the first time since Josh had known him, Nick gave an actual whisper: "Josh, it's time for us to go."

Nick stood and reached into the center of his long red robes to pull out an equally long matching red sack. He opened the sack on the floor and beckoned Josh to get inside it.

Josh placed both his sandaled feet into the center of the bag, and then Nick lifted the sides. The bag enlarged to cover Josh's legs, loincloth, muscled torso, brown beard, face, and finally, the crown of needles atop his head.

Nick tied a rope cord to seal the sack, and Josh instinctively balled himself up, hugging his arms around his folded knees and tucking his head into them.

He heard a small squeak as Nick opened the metal laundry chute door from behind the nursing station countertop. Josh remembered it as a nearly two-foot by two-foot square at about waist height above the floor. There was a soft rustle of velvet against metal as he surmised Nick was entering the laundry chute, then he felt the bag lift, with him within it, and he was somehow pulled up and forwards, then down into the dark chute below.

The metal door to the laundry chute must have been spring-loaded because it squeaked again as it shut behind them. The red bag was musty and stuffy and offered little protection from the dust and stale air in the long metal tunnel, forcing Josh to work hard to stop a sneeze. Then he heard a soft whisper from below.

"Hey Josh, do you know what happens when an elf falls asleep after drinking a cup of my special hot chocolate?"

"Nick." Josh bit his finger to calm himself, then whispered, "Seriously Nick, not now, please don't distract yourself!"

"Ho, ho, ho. Ha, ha ha!" The sack vibrated up and down in sync with each of Nick's heavy belly laughs. "Wrong answer, little fella."

Josh felt a jolt of acceleration, then a quick stop.

"Why, they have sweet dreams, of course!" Nick had stopped whispering, and his voice now echoed in the tube.

The movement pattern, a short fall followed by a controlled stop, repeated as Nick descended with Josh, one level, then another, and another, and more.

December on 5C4

XIV

THE CONTRACTIONS GREW STRONGER and closer together as Nick helped Josh descend farther down the canal of the laundry chute. Near the end, the canal curved horizontally into a deceleration track. Nick crawled out first, with an inexplicable effortlessness given his girth. The red bag stuck in the curve of the shaft. Josh pushed out slowly, headfirst and face down, then rotated sideways to pop out one shoulder, then another, then he slid out the rest of his body quickly.

The laundry chute ended on a large wooden table. Everything was so very dark. Josh lay on the table and could feel Nick standing above him. Nick reached over and into the chute canal to tug at the cord of the big red sack. Josh rested, Nick tugged, and, after a while, the large red bag tumbled forth. Josh could smell Nick's sweat and hear him breathing heavily.

"That—" Nick breathed in and out several times before catching his breath. "That, dear Josh, was quite a labor and delivery. Very laborious, which makes sense, as you are an impressive delivery."

"I agree," Josh said with a giggle which turned into a belly laugh. "When I talk about being reborn, I never imagine it this way, so thank you." He grabbed Nick's forearm and lifted himself into a sitting position atop the large landing table. His legs dangled over the tabletop and then one foot hit what he suspected was a large wicker basket. There was an odd clank of metal on glass, and Josh hopped down off the table to investigate.

"How do you mean it? How can someone be reborn after they've already been born the first time?" Nick asked. "They can't enter their mother's womb a second time to be born again."

Josh kneeled and felt around in the darkness. The wicker laundry basket was upside down beneath the large wooden table. He lifted the basket and felt the outline of an old kerosene hurricane lantern. He raised the lantern by the bail and, judging by the weight of it and the sloshing in the tank, it had some fuel.

Josh answered Nick, "Flesh gives birth to flesh, but spirit gives birth to spirit. *Reborn, born again*, it doesn't translate well—perhaps I'd do better saying *born from above*. We've all had our one and only physical birth, but our spirits can be born and reborn again and again." Josh reached under the laundry basket, this time with his other hand, and found a small metal box, which he shook to hear the rattling of what he presumed were matches.

"How can that be?"

"It's as simple as light." Josh stood up and placed the lantern on the wooden table. With two hands, he opened the box, grabbed a match, and struck it against the coarse strip on the side of a package. Fire. He raised the globe of the lantern with the thumb lever, exposed the wick, and lit it. The wick brightened and then dimmed to glow softly out from the frosted globe of the lantern. Josh continued, "Our souls burst forth and shine for all eternity. Being *reborn*, or *born from above*, or *born of the Spirit*, is when God's light—the love, compassion, and energy of God—flows unhindered through our souls and so through us out into the world around us."

"Can anyone be reborn?"

"Not just anyone—*everyone*." The God voice stirred inside Josh and sang him a short song, which he then chanted to Nick, "*If you want to change the reflection you see in the mirror each morn', I mean it's just your election, to vote for a chance to be reborn.*"

Josh lifted the lantern above his head and admired the soft light. He considered the song he just heard from the God voice. "My people teach that the tiniest light defeats even the most tremendous darkness. Each of us—we are the light of the world. A city on a hill cannot be hidden. Neither do people light a lantern like this one and put it under a laundry basket. Instead, they put it on a stand, where it gives light to everyone in the house. In the same way, we each need to let our light shine before others, so they can see our good deeds and give glory to God."

As he spoke, Josh held the bail of the lantern in his hand and swooped the light in a small circle around the center of the room. This small room was exactly as he had remembered it from when he volunteered with the laundry during his last hospital admission. It was a small antechamber for receiving soiled linens and towels from the laundry chute above. The chute itself curved and then opened onto a very large wooden table against one wall, where Josh and Nick had first landed. The walls of the room were brick, painted over red, and there was a large metal door to either side. Josh remembered one as the entrance from the hallway and the other as the opening to the actual laundry room, where the washing, drying, and folding occurred. Besides the chute and the table, most of this smaller room was occupied by an enormous industrial-sized hot water heater. The old huge cylindrical tank absorbed nearly half the room.

Nick tried the handle of each metal door but neither budged. They both looked up. The ceilings were high, more than twelve feet at least. There was a single latched window just below the ceiling of one of the walls, which presumably opened outside onto the hospital grounds.

Nick pointed a white-gloved index finger up to that one lonely window. "Both doors are locked. I think our only way out is up." Nick pulled the large wooden table out from against its wall, at an angle, then he pushed it further until it aligned to the side of the opposite wall, the one with the window atop it. "That window looks to be more than two bodies or so height up there. How about I climb on this table, and then you climb on me, and then you can escape through the window. Maybe even pull me up with something from the yard afterward, too."

Nick steadied his torso with one hand on the hot water tank and the other on the wall, then swung his legs up onto the wooden tabletop. He bent his legs, then folded himself over until his full weight was on the surface, and slowly stood.

But then there was a large cracking sound. All four wooden table legs snapped off simultaneously. The wooden tabletop fell to the floor, and Nick fell on top of it. One of the metal bolts flew past Josh's cheek, barely missing him, then ricocheted, puncturing the hot water tank. Josh heard the sudden hissing of steam and turned around to see a puff of white smoke sputtering out from the tank.

"Nick! Are you okay?"

"I'm fine, but I think we're both fucked now." Nick propped his back against the wall and sat upon the wooden tabletop from the broken table, now directly abutting the floor. He was draped in his large red robe with the white trim, the tips of his black boots jutted out from the bottom, his white-gloved hands made fists to prop up his bearded chin, the white pom-pom tip of his triangular hat folded down over and above his brow.

Josh hung the lantern high on a pipe bending off from the water tank and into the center of the room. He sat himself down next to Nick. Despite his near-nakedness, he did not feel cold. He wore only his white towel loincloth, brown leather sandals, and the crown of branches and green needles, which somehow remained firmly fixed atop his head.

Both men stared up at the lantern, then stared forward at the wall, then down to the floor. They brooded quietly for a time and there was mostly silence, except for the hissing and sputtering of steam now leaking from the damage to the large water heater tank.

It was Josh who spoke first. "This reminds me so much of what happened to a rebbe my father once knew." Josh untied and then retied the leather straps of his sandals as he sat next to Nick. "He was a great teacher who lived alone in a shack way out in the countryside. A jeep drove by, and the driver said, 'Rebbe, there will be a flood—come with me, and you'll be saved.' The rebbe replied, 'No, that's okay, God will save me.' So the jeep left. It started to rain, and there was a great deal of flooding."

"Next, a boat arrived, and the captain said, 'Rebbe, this flooding will get worse—come with me, and you'll be saved.' The rebbe replied, 'No, that's okay, God will save me.' And so the boat left."

"It continued to rain, and the water level rose so high that the rebbe had to climb atop the roof of his shack. A helicopter flew down, and the pilot said, 'Rebbe, this is a huge flood—come with me, and you'll be saved.' The rebbe replied, 'No, that's okay, God will save me.' and so the helicopter left."

"In the end, the water level rose above the shack, and the rebbe drowned. His soul went to heaven, and there he confronted God: 'Dear God, why didn't you save me?' And God replied, 'I tried, you *meshugenah*. I sent you a jeep, a boat, even a helicopter. What more could I have done?'"

"Ho, ho, ho. Ha, ha, ha." Nick's familiar belly laugh echoed loudly in the small room. Josh joined him giggling of his own. They laughed together for a long while, then were both quiet together again, though now both smiling. The only sound was the hiss and sputter of steam from various broken pipes and metal surfaces of the large water heater tank nearby. A layer of steam was slowly descending from the ceiling, and the soft glow of the lantern light was slowly dimming.

It was Nick who spoke next. "What more can we do? I think it's hopeless."

"There is always hope. With God, all things are possible." Josh flipped one hand to his left side. "There is always hope." Then another hand to his right side, "Just as there is always prayer."

Nick stopped staring straight ahead and turned to meet Josh in the eyes. "Can you teach me to pray?"

"Sure. It's easy. Easier than you'd think." Josh placed both hands flat together, then unfolded them in a pantomime of opening a book. "God's favorite prayers are the ones you offer to Him when you're alone, unseen by others, maybe in your room with a door closed. God sees everything and knows what's in your heart, so a great prayer is usually a simple prayer." Josh was beginning to sweat from all the heat and humidity growing in the small room. The muscles of his arms and chest glistened from the moisture. "I have a favorite prayer I wrote myself. I'll chant each line, translate it, and then you can repeat that part after me."

Nick pulled off a white glove from his right hand, then clasped Josh's left hand and interlaced their fingers together. They continued sitting next to one

December on 5C4

another and staring, mostly above them now, mostly at the cloud of steam descending from the ceiling and filling the center of the small room.

Josh squeezed Nick's hand, "This is how you should pray:

> ***Avee'nu sheashama'yeem,***
> Our Father, who art in heaven,
>
> ***Yeetkadesh sheemkah.***
> Hallowed be thy name.
>
> ***Tavo malchootey'cha,***
> Thy kingdom come,
>
> ***Yeaseh retzonekah***
> Thy will be done
>
> ***Kevashama'yeem ken Ba ah'retz***
> on earth as it is in heaven.
>
> ***Et le'chem chukenu ten la'nu haiyom***
> Give us this day our daily bread.
>
> ***Ooselach la'nu al chatael'nu,***
> And forgive us our debts,
>
> ***Kemo shesolecheem gam anach'nu lachoteem la'nu.***
> As we forgive our debtors.
>
> ***Veal teveeel'noo leedei neesayon,***
> And lead us not into temptation,
>
> ***Kee eem chaletzel'nu meen hara:***
> but deliver us from evil:
>
> ***Kee lecha hamalacha,***
> For thine is the kingdom,
>
> ***vehagevurah vehateefe'ret,***
> and the power, and the glory,
>
> ***leolemei olameem,***
> forever and ever,
>
> ***amein.***
> amen."

Josh translated aloud each line, then waited as Nick repeated it back to him. As they shared a final *amen* in unison, their affirmation was drowned out. The random hissing and sputtering of steam from the injured hot water heater transformed suddenly into a loud, angelic chorus of toots and whistles. Josh smelled burning rubber and metal. A growing cloud of hot steam surrounded them until, in an instant—after a sudden deep vibrating boom—the large water tank exploded, and a flood of water engulfed them.

XV

Hot turbid water filled the small room, forcefully, but then cooled, rapidly, as it abutted the cold brick walls. The lantern hanging above them had survived the explosion, and even remained lit. It cast a soft glow which reflected off the water's opaque surface. The small room now held a small lake. Its water level continued rising, above the men's waists, then beyond, but Josh somehow rose with it, and even above it!

*Are my feet on top of that broken tabletop? Is it floating upwards beneath the water line? Am I walking on that wood—*Josh tapped his feet on the surface beneath him—*Or am I walking on the water itself?*

He could feel no difference, and would a difference matter anyway? He stood upon the water's surface and walked steadily toward the small high window as the water level in the room continued its rapid rise.

Nick meanwhile was treading water feverishly beneath him. He looked up at Josh with his eyes and mouth wide open in amazement. "How is this possible? How can you walk on water? You are like a ghost! Should I be afraid?"

For Josh, the stench of burnt rubber and metal was somehow replaced by the scent of pine and roses. He saw a white glow through the small window as he walked toward it, and he heard chimes ringing from just beyond it. But he also made out Nick calling to him from below. "Nick, be of good cheer; it's just me, Josh, don't be afraid."

"I'm not a good swimmer, Josh." Nick's look of amazement was replaced by a countenance of fear and panic. "Can you help me walk on the water like you?"

"Come." Josh reached down and grabbed hold of Nick's hand. Nick immediately stopped flailing as he rose up from the water. Josh's eyes were fixed in a calm trance, his face utterly relaxed. Nick now stood above the water level, upon the water's surface, or maybe it was upon that large floating wooden tabletop. It was impossible to tell as the water was too cloudy, and it was all happening much too fast. Nick walked steadily towards Josh, as Josh walked steadily towards the window, the water itself now having filled up the small room near to its entirety.

Josh opened the latch of the glass window, and it blew open from a strong burst of wind laced with snowflakes. Josh crawled out through the open window first, but the blast of air startled Nick awake from his fugue. "Lord, save me!" Nick sunk back down beneath the water's surface, or perhaps it was just that he had stepped off the edge of the floating tabletop.

Josh stretched forth his hands through the window and took hold of both of Nick's hands. He repeated aloud as the God voice spoke to him, "O ye of little faith, why did you doubt?" And in that instant, the wind ceased, and the outside air stilled entirely. Josh tugged Nick up easily, out and through the window.

"Truly, Josh, truly you are miraculous!" Nick cried out in relief.

The two men lay beside each other on the back hospital lawn outside the open window. Stars twinkled. The fat man in a red velvet robe with white fur lining, white gloves, black boots, and a pointed red hat with a white pom-pom now lay next to the short, thin, muscled man wearing nothing but a towel loincloth, brown leather sandals and a crown of green branches. The two were wet; the two were cold; but the two were *free*.

Or nearly free?

They both lifted their heads to see a high red brick wall bordering the hospital's backyard.

The night sky was dark with no moon. There were clouds, but many patches of stars broke through from above. In the East, Josh saw again that large bright star he first had seen back in the hospital courtyard a few hours earlier. It seemed to have tripled in size from his last viewing, and rather than blinking and dimming, it was now one constant, steady flare. Josh pointed upwards at the miracle, to show Nick, then he offered the traditional blessing for seeing such a wonder: "**Barukh ata Adonai Eloheinu, melekh ha'olam, o'seh ma'ase be'reshit.**" *Blessed are You, Lord our God, King of the universe, Who re-enacts the work of creation.*

From what could be seen of the gated backyard of the hospital, in the present darkness, the whole area was apparently under construction. A large, dimly lit sign posted in the center of the lawn read *Kinneret Landscaping and Construction*. A thin dusty layer of snow lay everywhere; beneath it was a random array of hoes, shovels, dirtbags, turf rolls, flower pots, various bushes and trees in planter boxes, and different sorts of irrigation hoses and tubes.

Nearby, against the hospital wall, a wooden garden shed was clearly under construction. The outline was framed in lumber, and two completed central crossbeams were leaning nearby against the outside hospital wall.

Nick was quick to point them out. "I don't see a ladder, but we could drag those cross beams over to the brick wall, climb up them, and then jump over and finally be free. "

"Yes, Nick, take up a cross and follow me." Josh slowly stood up and then backed into a cross beam. He extended out his arms and wrapped them around the T bar of one of the crossbeams, then hunched forward with his head and his crown of needles turned downward, dragging the cross slowly behind him as he trudged across the lawn.

Being much larger, Nick lifted his cross from the base like a large battle ax and slung it over his shoulder. He then ran forward across the yard, quickly passing Josh. He angled his wooden crossbeam against the base of the brick wall and then, with a running start, pranced upward on the primary beam, jumped, then sat straddled over the edge of gray concrete flagstones marking the top of the brick wall.

Josh bore his cross with great solemnity. He steadily slid it across the yard. At the yard's edge, he angled his wooden crossbeam between the ground and the brick wall. Then, rather than run up the primary beam, Josh lay with his back on top of it, crossed his legs beneath his loincloth, and pushed upwards slowly with his feet. He grabbed each side of his crossbeam with his arms and pushed up there, too, splaying his arms out and his body open to the stars, all in a T formation atop the cross.

His crown of thorns rested firmly upon his head. He was exhausted and paused to rest. He lay upon his cross and looked up at Nick sitting on the edge of the wall. Behind him, between the clouds above, that odd star in the East continued to flame. Josh focused on the star until, somehow, its fire turned into a ray of white light. Josh watched as the light beamed down from the heavens and illuminated his body on the cross.

He saw only white, but now, with a different kind of sight, he witnessed everything, everywhere, and everywhen, all at once. He smelled the aroma of fresh baked bread and honey. A choir of euphonious angels sang to him above a melodious symphony. The God voice then spoke to Josh, *"For whoever wants to save their life will lose it, but whoever loses their life for Me will find it."* A deep, loving, mellifluous voice engulfed him. *"What good will it be for someone to gain the whole world, yet forfeit their soul? What can anyone give in exchange for their soul?"*

Josh understood now that his journey was at an end. He closed his eyes and sang the **Birkat Hagomel**, an ancient prayer to thank God after a dangerous journey. **"Baruch ata Adonai, Eloheinu melech ha-olam, ha-gomel l'chayavim tovot she-g'malani kol tov."** *Blessed are You, Lord our God, ruler of the world, who rewards the undeserving with goodness and who has rewarded me with goodness.* The choir of angels respond as Josh's **minyan**, **"Mi she-g'malcha kol tov, hu yi-**

g'malcha kol tov selah." May he who rewarded you with all goodness reward you with all goodness forever.

"Josh, come on, stop lying there, let's move it." Nick reached down a hand to Josh from the top of the wall.

And in that instant, the light, the music, the voices, it all evaporated for Josh. He startled, as if awakened from a dream, then looked up to Nick. "I have to go back. I have to go back in!" Josh yelled. "I don't want to save my life, and I don't want to lose my life. I don't want to gain the world; I don't want to forfeit my soul, and souls can't be exchanged." The vision was gone, but he could still smell the fresh bread and honey. "Our souls are immortal, but each of us can still choose an ordinary mortal life. It doesn't have to be perfect, just good enough." Josh sat up upon his leaning cross, slid his feet down, and stood on the ground far beneath Nick. "I just want to live; here and now."

That odd star in the East no longer burned. It flickered faintly, then faded to black.

"But I also need to go back. The order of the story, my story, it's all mixed up. It's not happening in the right order, and so it's all wrong. The pieces are all jumbled. It's not supposed to have happened this way." A strong wind rose and encircled Josh. "After I live this life now, my soul can go back and do it all again. But this time, in the right order. And at the right time. My story should have started a thousand years ago, maybe two, maybe a bit more."

Josh placed both hands over his heart. "Everyone needs me, everywhere and everywhen. But I'm not God—I can't be everywhere and everywhen, I'm still just a man." Josh arced an arm upwards over his head and pointed beyond the brick wall. "The world, that world outside, out there, it belongs to all of us." He rotated the same arm down and pointed back toward the hospital. "That world inside, that world in the hospital, that world belongs to me. I need it. I know that now."

Nick called down to Josh from atop the brick wall. "But if you go back, they'll force you to take your medication, that injection, the new long-acting version." Nick's jocular voice became tearful and mournful. "It will take away the God voice from you forever."

Josh pointed up at Nick, "Yes." He circled his finger in the air. "So, you and everyone else will have to listen for me." Josh stared into Nick's eyes. "It's your purpose. You, all of you, become like one body, with eyes and ears to witness compassion and hands and feet to do good works." Then he turned away from Nick to walk steadily in the dust of snow back to the hospital building.

Nick jumped down and escaped over the red brick wall. "Hey, Josh!" As he ran off, Nick called to Josh from behind the wall. "Do you know what they call an elf who finds his purpose?!" Nick paused only briefly, then hollered back the answer: "They call them *elf-actualized*!" A deep belly laugh echoed off the brick wall and down the city street. "Ho, ho, ho. Ha, ha, ha!"

Josh smiled as he arrived at the back of the hospital. He walked up several gray stone stairs to a wooden door under an archway. It was unlocked, and the knob turned. Before he opened it, he looked up one last time at the night sky. There was no trace of that peculiar star in the East. But just below where it had faded, he now saw a small red dot—maybe a helicopter—turning and twisting in upward spirals as it flew through the sky above. He thought he even heard a voice, maybe Nick's, somewhere far out in the distance. It was bellowing and laughing, but the words made no sense to Josh, "To the top of the porch! To the top of the wall! Now dash away! Dash away! Dash away all!"

XVI

NICK KEPT HIS PROMISE.

The next morning, on Josh's birthday, piles of wrapped gifts with bows appeared under that fir tree in the central courtyard of the hospital. They each had a small card attached, with the recipient's name and a closing "From Mr. K," in distinctive silver cursive lettering.

It was an unexplained spectacle and, for Josh, the finale of a long series of odd occurrences. That morning nobody had any hot water, yet everybody had a present—most of the boxes were filled with wooden toys or plush dolls of one sort or another. There were gifts not just for the patients but for the staff, too: Dr. Fischman, Roy, even Ms. Longhini. Nick had gifted her with new glasses and a loud coach whistle on a gold necklace.

Josh was given a small box they had found addressed to him. It had a more personal note: "Dear Josh, Happy Birthday! Keep these for later, you'll need them soon. Hugs and Love, Nick." Inside the box were two simple silver rings. Josh closed this present, left it on his cot, then walked over to the nursing station for his second present—his shot—from Ms. Longhini herself: 819 milligrams of antipsychotic depot medication in a 2.625 cubic centimeter intramuscular injection.

He made one last wish, sat down, received the shot, then stood up.

The onset of action was as rapid as the delivery.

Just like that, Josh was alone. Just like that, the only voice he would ever hear in his head again would be his own. Just like that, Josh's adventure ended so his story could finally begin.

Later that morning, as Josh was strolling in the snowy courtyard during outdoor time, Roy approached him. "Josh, you have a visitor." He took out a clipboard with a piece of paper for Josh to sign. "Will you accept a visit from someone named Judah?"

"I don't know him, but I welcome everyone." He managed to sign the form despite his hands trembling from the new drug.

Roy walked Josh back through the main hospital, then into ward 5C4,

December on 5C4

and on into their common room. A thin man with short curly red hair sat there awaiting him. He wore a blue visitor name tag imprinted with "Judah I."

"Yehud!" Josh cried, "I am so sorry for so many things. I'm ready to change." They rushed up to each other, and the two embraced. There was a large, long, open-mouthed kiss.

A round cake with thirty-three small candles was on a table. "I'm sorry too, Josh. And I'm ready to change, also. I'm ready to change a lot of things." Yehud—now Judah—took a lighter and lit the candles. "I finally took a ***goyim*** name, like you. It's about time, I think."

Josh pressed his fingers onto Yehud's name tag. "*Judah*. I like it." Josh closed his eyes. "I think it's about time, too." He blew out his candles. "Let's go back to building houses, including our own."

XVII

I T WAS PERHAPS A DECADE or more later before Josh ever met Nick again, if he had ever really met him at all.

Josh and Judah stood together, leaning their backs against their parked white truck, both staring watchfully into the inside of the grocery store. Jessica was committed to baking Josh a cake for his birthday tomorrow and wanted to do it 'all by herself,' not just the baking but also the buying of all the ingredients she would need in the store. They were proud parents of a proud ten-year-old daughter, whom they had raised to be as stubborn and self-sufficient as she was loving and kind.

The two men matched. They wore matching polo shirts, each stamped with their company insignia—*J&J Construction*—which was also emblazoned on both sides of their truck. They had matching middle-aged bellies folded over matching work jeans. They clasped their hands together and their intertwined fingers revealed matching silver rings.

Flurries fell from the sky to scatter across the parking lot. A young red-haired girl with two small bags of groceries approached the two men. *"Tatis, ken ikh hobn gelt tsu gebn dem man?"* Daddies, may I have money to give to that man?

"What man?" Judah asked.

"Der mentsh mit dem glok." Jessica pointed to a man with a bell on the sidewalk in front of the grocery store. He was a tall, fat man dressed in a red velvet robe with white fur trim, he wore a matching triangular cap with a white pom-pom and a set of shiny black boots. He had just set up a tall metal tripod that held a red metal bucket hanging from its center. He smiled and rang a large bell—a silver metal cup and clapper set on a long wooden handle. The man erupted with a deep belly laugh, "Ho, ho, ho. Ha, ha, ha." To Josh, this all seemed so familiar, so recognizable… yet somehow so indiscernible.

Jessica reverted to *goyishe shprakh*. "Daddies, there is a sign in big silver writing that says he is raising money for the poor—for groceries and toys for families in need. Can we donate?" Judah lifted the bags from Jessica and placed them into the back of their truck. Josh opened his wallet and gave her a bill. His thumb rolled back and forth against his fingers with a small tremor.

Jessica walked back to the big, jolly man. She paused near the line of grocery store carts and briefly watched him ring his bell and laugh. Then she walked over and dropped the bill into his red metal kettle. The man stopped laughing and ringing for a time. He bent down on one knee and chatted with Jessica. Soon afterward, she turned around and darted back to join Josh and Judah waiting in the parking lot. The fat man stood up and returned to laughing and ringing his bell.

"What a silly man, but he has such kind eyes." Jessica climbed into the front seat and strapped in between Judah and Josh.

"What did he say to you?" Judah grabbed a green pear from a bag on the dashboard, took a bite, then started the engine.

"He thanked me, then asked me a riddle."

"Oh really?" Josh closed his eyes and reached inward toward a distant memory, but then it vanished like a dream, "What was the riddle?"

"How do elves celebrate their birthdays?" Jessica held up both thumbs and index fingers one inch apart to animate the query.

Josh peered at the big man's reflection in the rearview window as Judah backed the truck out of the parking space. Kind eyes stared back at him. Josh took his hand and rubbed it over the recent injection site on his arm. Then he placed the palms of each hand one atop the other, with several inches between them. "They bake shortcakes!"

"How'd you know?" Jessica giggled.

Josh smiled.

Acknowledgments

I AM EXTRAORDINARILY GRATEFUL to B.S.Roberts and the entire Nat 1 Publishing team. They were willing to place a rather odd gamble on this rather eccentric holiday tale written by this rather weird older man.

I retired in 2019 from my career as a psychiatrist, intending to dedicate the second half of my life to writing fiction. The COVID pandemic upended these plans. But then, as life slowly returned to our new normal, we shared a first family outing—masked and socially distanced—to the town of Leavenworth, Washington. A Christmas village! There, I was inspired to write a short story that outgrew itself over and over again until it became this novella here today.

I remembered many stories from my residency years, some apocryphal, some accurate, of involuntary hospitalizations of various patients with delusions of being either Jesus or Santa. It occurred to me it would be interesting to see what might happen if a patient with similarities to Jesus were hospitalized concurrently with a patient with similarities to Santa. Would they be friends? Enemies? Both? And thus emerged *December on 5C4*.

I want to thank all of my family and friends for their patience with me as I snuck away to write this novella. I am grateful too to all the communities of faith of which I have been a part: Monsey Jewish Center, Harvard Hillel, Stanford Hillel, Unity Palo Alto, First Congregational Church of Palo Alto, Westminster Presbyterian Church of Portland, and others yet to come. I also am indebted to the many medical communities where I trained and worked: Stanford University School of Medicine, Stanford Medical Center, the Stanford University Department of Psychiatry and Behavioral Sciences, the Cowell Student Health Center at Stanford, the Menlo Park Veterans Association Hospital, Palo Alto Veterans Association Hospital, with a special thanks to the compassionate doctors, nurses, and staff of the real locked ward 5C4 of the 1990s. Finally, I am forever beholden to Arriba Juntos in San Francisco and the Police and Fire Departments of Redwood City, where I had the privilege of volunteering as a community Santa for a great many years.

All these paths I have walked, and all have made me the writer I am today.

Please celebrate the seasons however you celebrate them—and most especially, may you have a wonderful winter holiday!

About the Author

ADAM STRASSBERG is a retired psychiatrist living in Portland, Oregon. He uses the intersection of psychology, religion, mythology, and magical realism to explore the human condition through fiction. His stories have been published in *Fiction on the Web*, *Cafe Lit*, *Total Quality Reading*, *Please See Me,* other online portals, and various print magazines and anthologies. When not writing or napping, he can be found updating his website at www.adamstrassberg.com

Further praise for December on 5C4

December on 5C4 begins in *medias res*, leaving the reader disoriented along with the narrator until the situation grows clearer. But a patient in a mental hospital is not a reliable narrator, so a delightful fog overlays the story which may or may not be categorized as magical realism. It depends on how much you believe in Jesus and Santa. They are unlikely friends in terms of temperament: Josh is a tortured soul, trying to reconcile his identity with his religion, while Topher is a jolly and joyful man with his struggles more carefully hidden. Both men are trying to make a positive impact on the world--the whole world--and that is where they come together.

— Elise Shumock, the Book Publican of the Rose City Book Pub

•••

Adam Strassberg takes your standard vanilla Christmas tale from the deep freeze, cuts it into unique shapes, and decorates it with an exuberant hand. Whether describing a cocaine-addled Santa or a delusional Jesus, his empathy for his imperfect characters shines through on every page. What results is a richly detailed account of life in a psych ward that's also unexpectedly sweet and wholesome.

— Andrew Fort, HOCUS Grand Scribe and author of *The Emerald Ballroom*

•••

With humor and an underlying, earnest theological underpinning, this story touches on big themes: economic inequalities, the meaning of community, mental illness, homelessness, and centrally, peacemaking and unconditional love. A good, clever, enjoyable read!

— Laurie Lynn Newman, M.A., M.Div.

•••

A gripping, gutsy, and utterly original story!

— Adam Dorsay, Psy. D., Author of *Super Psyched*

•••

Adam Strassberg has written an enchanting story, combining stories of Christianity, Judaism, and Santa with a healthy dose of magical realism to create a lovely snow globe of holiday cheer and spiritualism. I found it to be very uplifting and inclusive, and it's a gem for readers, no matter what their backgrounds or belief systems are. Well done! I look forward to reading more from this debut author.

— Melissa Usack, Librarian, Innovative Interfaces

Holiday drama coming up, featuring Christmas psychiatry in Hebrew, in the recovery ward. So wash your face. Have breakfast. Help the homeless. God is talking. Spiritual transformation. It's a fun read. Check it out.

— John Angell Grant, Playwright, Poet, and Author of *The Green Notebook*

•••

Delightfully intriguing! You think you know what is going to happen, and then....it twists!

— Robin Rolfe, Librarian, Portland Public Schools

•••

Lost on the urban December streets, homeless Joshua navigates the boundary between the intransigence of his own religious fervor and capitalist disdain for what he has become, all the while suffering a mental health crisis that is alternately a blessing and a curse. In this "what if" parable for the present day, our tortured hero lands once again in a psychiatric ward known only as 5C4. But this time, he meets toymaker Nick. And together, they make choices that surprise the reader at every turn. On all fronts, author and retired psychiatrist Adam Strassberg knows whereof he speaks. *December on 5C4* is a small gem of a read, sure to spur discussion well beyond the Christmas season!

— Carol Stivers, Author of *The Mother Code*

•••

Here's why everyone who has struggled with religious identity, emotional pain, or the holidays should read *December on 5C4:* Through lively storytelling, it brings deep humanity to the struggles of mental illness, blending Jewish wisdom and progressive Christian theology, as well as history and magic realism, into a wonderful story of hope and recovery.

` — Eli Merrit, M.D., Doctor and Historian, Vanderbilt University, Author of *Disunion Among Ourselves*

•••

December on 5C4 is an original, entertaining, moving, and even enlightening tale of psychic, spiritual, and personal discovery.

— Ethan Herschenfeld, Actor and Comedian "Thug Thug Jew"

Jesus and Santa compare notes while cooling their heels in a psych ward. This fascinating premise is core to *December on 5C4* and Strassberg cleverly navigates the theology and psychology of this mythical encounter.

Rather than simply mashing-up the two personalities and their complex histories, Strassberg extracts the parts necessary for his story, then inserts them into current events. Jesus becomes a homeless encampment leader. Strassberg places Santa in the here-and-now while keeping his mystical essence intact. This gives Strassberg the room needed to explore how these two would compare their world-views.

This isn't a casual read; expect to parse religion and ethics. But the story maintains cohesion and the reader will find themselves rewarded at the end.

— Mark Niemann-Ross, author of *Stupid Machine*

•••

A sweet story of two legendary characters just a little out of sync with the stories we know, thrown together by circumstance and mental illness. Writing with sympathy and understanding, Strassberg pays homage to the holidays with rollicking aplomb.

— Michael Allen Rose, Author of *Jurassichrist*

•••

In *December on 5C4*, Adam Strassberg cleverly examines the cultural symbolism of Jesus and Santa, shedding light on the social forces shaping our holiday values. By contrasting sacred and secular icons, the narrative explores themes of consumerism, faith, generosity, houselessness, humility, mental health, and moral responsibility. It prompts readers to consider how these figures reflect and challenge our modern society's priorities, inviting us all to take a deeper look at the true spirit of the season. This compelling, insightful, well-crafted novella brings sociology into the very heart of holiday storytelling. It's a holiday tale with a scholarly edge."

— Tomas Jimenez, Ph.D., Professor of Sociology, Stanford University

•••

As an uncertified therapist, and as a certified human, I recommend *December on 5C4* with my whole *Gestalt*.

— Dr. Samuel Benjamin, Author of *Today is Now!*

•••

Author Adam Strassberg uses a modern-day psych ward meeting between Jesus and Santa to give us a mystical and magical modern-day myth about love, humanity and redemption. Strassberg dazzles us with a street-smart, holy and heart-filled glimpse into a world where God tells knock-knock jokes and hands out pears. Give yourself a gift and read this novella!

— Todd Erickson, author, *Baxter and Jeffrey* and *Freya Takes Charge*

December on 5C4 is a profound and imaginative tale that seamlessly blends the realities of mental illness with the rich symbolism of two enduring cultural and spiritual figures: Jesus Christ and Santa Claus. As a therapist, I was deeply moved by the authenticity of its portrayal of life in a psychiatric hospital and the compassionate exploration of trauma, recovery, and identity. Josh and Nick's journey is an extraordinary metaphor for the human struggle to reconcile pain with purpose, drawing on the self-sacrifice and redemption of Jesus and the generosity and healing spirit of Santa. This novella captures the transformative power of friendship, the courage required for self-acceptance, and the magic that emerges when belief—whether in oneself or in others—is nurtured. It's a deeply insightful and heartwarming story that offers both hope and reflection, making it a must-read for anyone interested in the intersections of mental health, spirituality, and human connection.

— Brittney Chesworth, Ph.D., Author of *Help! I'm Dying Again*

•••

December on 5C4 effectively intersects mental well-being and religious spirituality without evangelizing people to one faith or another. Instead, Adam Strassberg invites readers to consider their own relationships to their mental health, spirituality, and identity as a whole in times that call for resilience and vulnerability. While taking place in the cold setting of 5C4, its warm themes of community, self-acceptance, and hope take precedence and safely bring readers along Josh's journey of transformation. Touching on important and more than contemporarily relevant issues facing intergenerational communities, December on 5C4 is an engaging read not only for the holidays, but for those with an interest in bridging their faiths and spiritualities with their mental, spiritual, and communal health.

— Junha Kim, Director of Youth, Mission, and Community Engagement at Westminster Presbyterian Portland

•••

Adam Strassberg dives into the deep end of human experience. He is unafraid of any subject, especially the ones most of us avoid: religion, sex, politics, money, mental health, and our deepest fears about who we are. In *December on 5C4*, Adam reinterprets common mythology with humor and depth, inviting us to understand mental illness and our shared stories in a new way. You might experience him as either a dangerous heretic or an insightful oracle. I think he may be both.

— Rev. David Howell, Senior Minister, First Congregational Church of Palo Alto, UCC

•••

Thought-provoking and magical. Full of humor, pain, and insight.

— Felicity Niven, Author of *Convergence of Desire*

Made in United States
Troutdale, OR
12/03/2024